FALLING FOR THE SECRET MILLIONAIRE

BY

KATE HARDY

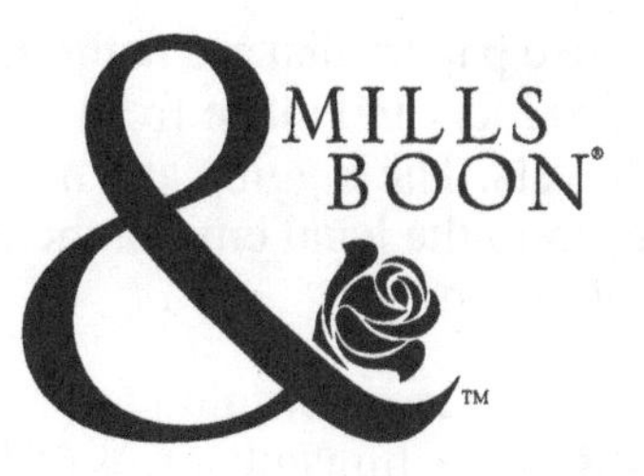

First published in Great Britain 2016
By Mills & Boon, an imprint of HarperCollins*Publishers*
1 London Bridge Street, London, SE1 9GF

Large Print edition 2016

ISBN: 978-0-263-26269-8

Our policy is to use papers that are natural, renewable and recyclable products and made from wood grown in sustainable forests. The logging and manufacturing processes conform to the legal environmental regulations of the country of origin.

Printed and bound in Great Britain
by CPI Antony Rowe, Chippenham, Wiltshire

FALLING FOR THE SECRET MILLIONAIRE

For my friend Sherry Lane, with love
(and thanks for not minding me
sneaking research stuff into our trips
out with the girls!).
xxx

CHAPTER ONE

'ARE YOU ALL RIGHT, Miss Thomas?' the lawyer asked.

'Fine, thank you,' Nicole fibbed. She was still trying to get her head round the news. The grandfather she'd never met—the man who'd thrown her mother out on the street when he'd discovered that she was pregnant with Nicole and the father had no intention of marrying her—had died and left Nicole a cinema in his will.

A run-down cinema, from the sounds of it; the solicitor had told her that the place had been closed for the last five years. But, instead of leaving the place to benefit a charity or someone in the family he was still speaking to, Brian Thomas had left the cinema to her: to the grandchild he'd rejected before she'd even been born.

Why?

Guilt, because he knew he'd behaved badly and should've been much more supportive to his only daughter? But, if he'd wanted to make amends, surely he would've left the cinema to Nicole's mother? Or was this his way to try to drive a wedge between Susan and Nicole?

Nicole shook herself. Clearly she'd been working in banking for too long, to be this cynical about a stranger's motivations.

'It's actually not that far from where you live,' the solicitor continued. 'It's in Surrey Quays.'

Suddenly Nicole knew exactly what and where the cinema was. 'You mean the old Electric Palace on Mortimer Gardens?'

'You know it?' He looked surprised.

'I walk past it every day on my way to work,' she said. In the three years she'd been living in Surrey Quays, she'd always thought the old cinema a gorgeous building, and it was a shame that the place was neglected and boarded up. She hadn't had a clue that the cinema had any connection with her at all. Though there was a local history thread in the Surrey Quays forum—the local community website she'd joined when she'd first moved to her flat in Docklands—which included several posts about the Electric Palace's past. Someone had suggested setting up a volunteer group to get the cinema back up and running again, except nobody knew who owned it.

Nicole had the answer to that now. She was the new owner of the Electric Palace. And it was the last thing she'd ever expected.

'So you know what you're taking on, then,' the solicitor said brightly.

Taking on? She hadn't even decided whether to accept the bequest yet, let alone what she was going to do with it.

'Or,' the solicitor continued, 'if you don't want to take it on, there is another option. A local development company has been in touch with us, expressing interest in buying the site, should you wish to sell. It's a fair offer.'

'I need a little time to think this through before I make any decisions,' Nicole said.

'Of course, Miss Thomas. That's very sensible.'

Nicole smiled politely, though she itched to remind the solicitor that she was twenty-eight years old, not eight. She wasn't a naive schoolgirl, either: she'd worked her way up from the bottom rung of the ladder to become a manager in an investment bank. Sensible was her default setting. Was it not obvious from her tailored business suit and low-heeled shoes, and in the way she wore her hair pinned back for work?

'Now, the keys.' He handed her a bunch of ancient-looking keys. 'We will of course need time to alter the deeds, should you decide to keep it. Otherwise we can handle the conveyancing of the property, should you decide to sell to the developer or to someone else. We'll wait for your instructions.'

'Thank you,' Nicole said, sliding the keys into her handbag. She still couldn't quite believe she owned the Electric Palace.

'Thank you for coming in to see us,' the solicitor continued. 'We'll be in touch with the paperwork.'

She nodded. 'Thank you. I'll call you if there's anything I'm unsure about when I get it.'

'Good, good.' He gave her another of those avuncular smiles.

As soon as Nicole had left the office, she

grabbed her phone from her bag and called her mother—the one person she really needed to talk to about the bequest. But the call went straight through to Susan's voicemail. Then again, at this time of day her mother would be in a meeting or with one of her probationers. Nicole's best friend Jessie, an English teacher, was knee-deep in exam revision sessions with her students, so she wouldn't be free to talk to Nicole about the situation until the end of the day. And Nicole definitely didn't want to discuss this with anyone from work; she knew they'd all tell her to sell the place to the company who wanted to buy it, for the highest price she could get, and to keep the money.

Her head was spinning. Maybe she would sell the cinema—after all, what did she know about running a cinema, let alone one that hadn't been in operation for the last five years and looked as if it needed an awful lot of work doing to it before it could open its doors again? But, if she did sell the Electric Palace, she had no intention of keeping the money. As far as she was concerned, any money from Brian Thomas ought to go to his daughter, not skip a generation. Susan Thomas had spent years struggling as a single mother, working three jobs to pay the rent when Nicole was tiny. If the developer really was offering a fair price, it could give Susan the money to pay off her mortgage, go on a good holiday and buy a new car. Though Nicole knew she'd have to work hard to convince her mother that she deserved the money; plus Susan might be even more loath to accept anything from her father on the grounds that it was way too late.

Or Nicole could refuse the bequest on principle. Brian Thomas had never been part of her life or shown any interest in her. Why should she be interested in his money now?

She sighed. What she really needed right now was some decent caffeine and the space to talk this through with someone. There was only one person other than her mother and Jessie whose advice she trusted. Would he be around? She found the nearest coffee shop, ordered her usual double espresso, then settled down at a quiet table and flicked into the messaging program on her phone. Clarence was probably busy, but then again if she'd caught him on his lunch break he might have time to talk.

In the six months since they'd first met on the Surrey Quays forum, they'd become close and they talked online every day. They'd never actually met in person; and, right from the first time he'd sent her a private message, they'd agreed that they wouldn't share personal details that identified them, so they'd stuck to their forum names of Georgygirl and Clarence. She had no idea what he even looked like—she could have passed him in the street at any time during the three years she'd been living at Surrey Quays. In some ways it was a kind of coded, secret relationship, but at the same time Nicole felt that Clarence knew the real her. Not the corporate ghost who spent way too many hours in the office, or the much-loved daughter and best friend who was always nagged about working too hard, but the *real* Nicole. He knew the one who wondered about the universe and dreamed of the stars. Late at night, she'd told him things she'd never told anyone else, even her mother or Jessie.

Maybe Clarence could help her work out the right thing to do.

She typed a message and mentally crossed her fingers as she sent it.

Hey, Clarence, you around?

Gabriel Hunter closed his father's office door behind him and walked down the corridor as if he didn't have a care in the world.

What he really wanted to do was to beat his fists against the walls in sheer frustration. When, when, *when* was he going to stop paying for his teenage mistake?

OK, so it had been an awful lot worse than the usual teenage mistakes—he'd crashed his car into a shop front one night on the way home from a party and done a lot of damage. But nobody had been physically hurt and he'd learned his lesson immediately. He'd stopped going round with the crowd who'd thought it would be fun to spike his drink when he was their designated driver. He'd knuckled down to his studies instead of spending most of his time partying, and at the end of his final exams he'd got one of the highest Firsts the university had ever awarded. Since then, he'd proved his worth over and over again in the family business. Time after time he'd bitten his tongue so he didn't get into a row with his father. He'd toed the party line. Done what was expected of him, constantly repented for his sins to atone in his father's eyes.

And his father still didn't trust him. All Gabriel ever saw in his father's eyes was 'I saved you from yourself'. Was Evan Hunter only capable of seeing his son as the stupid teenager who got in with a bad crowd? Would he ever see Gabriel for who he was now, all these years later? Would he ever respect his son?

Days like today, Gabriel felt as if he couldn't breathe. Maybe it was time to give up trying to change his family's view of him and to walk away. To take a different direction in his career—though, right at that moment, Gabriel didn't have a clue what that would be, either. He'd spent the last seven years since graduation working hard in the family business and making sure he knew every single detail of Hunter Hotels Ltd. He'd tried so hard to do the right thing. The reckless teenager he'd once been was well and truly squashed—which he knew was a good thing, but part of him wondered what would have happened if he hadn't had the crash. Would he have grown out of the recklessness but kept his freedom? Would he have felt as if he was really worth something, not having to pay over and over for past mistakes? Would he be settled down now, maybe with a family of his own?

All the women he'd dated over the last five years saw him as Gabriel-the-hotel-chain-heir, the rich guy who could show them a good time and splash his cash about, and he hated that superficiality. Yet the less superficial, nicer women were wary of him, because his reputation got in the way; everyone knew that Gabriel Hunter was a former wild child and was now a ruthless company man, so he'd never commit emotionally and there was no point in dating him because there wasn't a future in the relationship. And his family all saw him as Gabe-who-made-the-big-mistake.

How ironic that the only person who really saw him for himself was a stranger. Someone whose real name he didn't even know, let alone what she did or what she looked like, because they'd been careful not to exchange those kinds of details. But over the last six months he'd grown close to Georgygirl from the Surrey Quays forum.

Which made it even more ironic that he'd only joined the website because he was following his father's request to keep an eye out for local disgruntled residents who might oppose the new Hunter Hotel they were developing from a run-down former spice warehouse in Surrey Quays, and charm them into seeing things the Hunter way. Gabriel had discovered that he liked the anonymity of an online persona—he could actually meet people and get to know them, the way he couldn't in real life. The people on the forum didn't know he was Gabriel Hunter, so they had no preconceptions and they accepted him for who he was.

He'd found himself posting on a lot of the same topics as someone called Georgygirl. The more he'd read her posts, the more he'd realised that she was on his wavelength. They'd flirted a bit—because an internet forum was a pretty safe place to flirt—and he hadn't been able to resist contacting her in a private message. Then they'd started chatting to each other away from the forum. They'd agreed to stick to the forum rules of not sharing personal details that would identify themselves, so Gabriel had no idea of Georgygirl's real name or her personal situation; but in their late-night private chats he felt that he could talk to her about anything and everything. Be his real self. Just as he was pretty sure that she was her real self with him.

Right now, it was practically lunchtime. Maybe Georgygirl would be around? He hoped so, because talking to her would make him feel human again. Right now he really needed a dose of her teasing sarcasm to jolt him out of his dark mood.

He informed his PA that he was unavailable for the next hour, then headed out to Surrey Quays. He ordered a double espresso in his favourite café, then grabbed his phone and flicked into the direct messaging section of the Surrey Quays forum.

And then he saw the message waiting for him.

Hey, Clarence, you around?

It was timed fifteen minutes ago. Just about when he'd walked out of that meeting and wanted to punch a wall. Hopefully she hadn't given up waiting for him and was still there. He smiled.

Yeah. I'm here, he typed back.

He sipped his coffee while he waited for her to respond. Just as he thought it was too late and she'd already gone, a message from her popped up on his screen.

Hello, there. How's your day?

I've had better, he admitted. You?

Weird.

Why?

Then he remembered she'd told him that she'd had a letter out of the blue from a solicitor she'd never heard of, asking her to make an appointment because they needed to discuss something with her.

What happened at the solicitor's?

I've been left something in a will.

That's good, isn't it?

Unless it was a really odd bequest, or one with strings.

It's property.

Ah. It was beginning to sound as if there were strings attached. And Gabriel knew without Georgygirl having to tell him that she was upset about it.

Don't tell me—it's a desert island or a ruined castle, but you have to live there for a year all on your own with a massive nest of scary spiders before you can inherit?

Not quite. But thank you for making me laugh.

Meaning that right now she wanted to cry?

What's so bad about it? Is it a total wreck that needs gutting, or it has a roof that eats money?

There was a long pause.

It needs work, but that isn't the bad thing. The bequest is from my grandfather.

Now he understood. The problem wasn't with what she'd been left: it was who'd left it to her that was the sticking point.

How can I accept anything from someone who let my mother down so badly?

She'd confided the situation to him a couple of months ago, when they'd been talking online late at night and drinking wine together—about how her mother had accidentally fallen pregnant, and when her parents had found out that her boyfriend was married, even though her mother hadn't had a clue that he wasn't single when they'd started dating, they had thrown her out on the street instead of supporting her.

Gabriel chafed every day about his own situation, but he knew that his family had always been there for him and had his best interests at heart, even if his father was a control freak who couldn't move on from the past. Georgygirl's story had made him appreciate that for the first time in a long while.

Maybe, he typed back carefully, this is his way of apologising. Even if it is from the grave.

More like trying to buy his way into my good books? Apart from the fact that I can't be bought, he's left it way too late. He let my mum struggle when she was really vulnerable. This feels like thirty pieces of silver. Accepting the bequest means I accept what he—and my grandmother—did. And I *don't*. At all.

He could understand that.

Is your grandmother still alive? Maybe you could go and see her. Explain how you feel. And maybe she can apologise on his behalf as well as her own.

I don't know. But, even if she is alive, I can't see her apologising. What kind of mother chucks her pregnant daughter into the street, Clarence? OK, so they were angry and hurt and shocked at the time—I can understand that. But my mum didn't know that my dad was married or she would never have dated him, much less anything else. And they've had twenty-nine years to get over it. As far as I know, they've never so much as seen a photo of me, let alone cuddled me as a baby or sent me a single birthday card.

And that had to hurt, being rejected by your family when they didn't even know you.

It's their loss, he typed. But maybe they didn't know how to get in touch with your mother.

Surely all you have to do is look up someone in the electoral roll, or even use a private detective if you can't be bothered to do it yourself?

That's not what I meant, Georgy. It's not the finding her that would've been hard—it's breaking the ice and knowing what to say. Sometimes pride gets in the way.

Ironic, because he knew he was guilty of that, too. Not knowing how to challenge his father—because how could you challenge someone when you were always in the wrong?

Maybe. But why leave the property to *me* and not to my mum? It doesn't make sense.

Pride again? Gabriel suggested. And maybe he thought it would be easier to approach you.

From the grave?

Could be Y-chromosome logic?

That earned him a smiley face.

Georgy, you really need to talk to your mum about it.

I would. Except her phone is switched to voice-mail.

Shame.

I know this is crazy, she added, but you were the one I really wanted to talk to about this. You see things so clearly.

It was the first genuine compliment he'd had in a long time—and it was one he really appreciated.

Thank you. Glad I can be here for you. That's what friends are for.

And they were friends. Even though they'd never met, he felt their relationship was more real and more honest than the ones in his real-life world—where ironically he couldn't be his real self.

I'm sorry for whining.

You're not whining. You've just been left something by the last person you expected to leave you anything. Of course you're going to wonder why. And if it is an apology, you're right that it's too little, too late. He should've patched up the row years ago and been proud of your mum for raising a bright daughter who's also a decent human being.

Careful, Clarence, she warned. I might not be able to get through the door of the coffee shop when I leave, my head's so swollen.

Coffee shop? Even though he knew it was ridiculous—this wasn't the only coffee shop in Surrey

Quays, and he had no idea where she worked so she could be anywhere in London right now—Gabriel found himself pausing and glancing round the room, just in case she was there.

But everyone in the room was either sitting in a group, chatting animatedly, or looked like a businessman catching up with admin work.

There was always the chance that Georgygirl was a man, but he didn't think so. He didn't think she was a bored, middle-aged housewife posing as a younger woman, either. And she'd just let slip that her newly pregnant mother had been thrown out twenty-nine years ago, which would make her around twenty-eight. His own age.

I might not be able to get through the door of the coffee shop, my head's so swollen.

Ha. This was the teasing, quick-witted Georgygirl that had attracted him in the first place. He smiled.

We need deflationary measures, then. OK. You need a haircut and your roots are showing. And there's a massive spot on your nose. It's like the red spot on Mars. You can see it from outer space.

Jupiter's the one with the red spot, she corrected. But I get the point. Head now normal size. Thank you.

Good.

And he just bet she knew he'd deliberately mixed up his planets. He paused.

Seriously, though—maybe you could sell the property and split the money with your mum.

It still feels like thirty pieces of silver. I was thinking about giving her all of it. Except I'll have to persuade her because she'll say he left it to me.

Or maybe it isn't an apology—maybe it's a rescue.

Rescue? How do you work that out? she asked.

You hate your job.

She'd told him that a while back—and, being in a similar situation, he'd sympathised.

If you split the money from selling the property with your mum, would it be enough to tide you over for a six-month sabbatical? That might give you enough time and space to find out what you really want to do. OK, so your grandfather wasn't there when your mum needed him—but right now it looks to me as if he's given you something that you need at exactly the right time. A chance for independence, even if it's only for a little while.

I never thought of it like that. You could be right.

It is what it is. You could always look at it as a belated apology, which is better than none at all. He wasn't there when he should've been, but he's come good now.

Hmm. It isn't residential property he left me.

It's a business?

Yes. And it hasn't been in operation for a while.

A run-down business, then. Which would take money and time to get it back in working order—the building might need work, and the stock or the fixtures might be well out of date. So he'd been right in the first place and the bequest had come with strings.

Could you get the business back up and running?

Though it would help if he knew what kind of business it actually was. But asking would be breaking the terms of their friendship—because then she'd be sharing personal details.

In theory, I could. Though I don't have any experience in the service or entertainment industry.

He did. He'd grown up in it.

That's my area, he said.

He was taking a tiny risk, telling her something personal—but she had no reason to connect Clarence with Hunter Hotels.

My advice, for what it's worth—an MBA and working for a very successful hotel chain, though he could hardly tell her that without her working out exactly who he was—is that staff are the key. Look at what your competitors are doing and offer your clients something different. Keep a close eye on your costs and income, and get advice from a business start-up specialist. Apply for all the grants you can.

It was solid advice. And Nicole knew that Clarence would be the perfect person to brainstorm ideas with, if she decided to keep the Electric Palace. She was half tempted to tell him everything—but then they'd be sharing details of their real and professional lives, which was against their agreement. He'd already told her too much by letting it slip that he worked in the service or entertainment industry. And she'd as good as told him her age. This was getting risky; it wasn't part of their agreement. Time to back off and change the subject.

Thank you, she typed. But enough about me. You said you'd had a bad day. What happened?

A pointless row. It's just one of those days when I feel like walking out and sending off my CV to half a dozen recruitment agencies. Except it's the family business and I know it's my duty to stay.

Because he was still trying to make up for the big mistake he'd made when he was a teenager? He'd told her the bare details one night, how he was the disgraced son in the family, and that he was never sure he'd ever be able to change their perception of him.

Clarence, maybe you need to talk to your dad or whoever runs the show in your family business about the situation and say it's time for you all to move on. You're not the same person now as you were when you were younger. Everyone makes mistakes—and you can't spend the rest of your life making up for it. That's not reasonable.

Maybe.

Clarence must feel as trapped as she did, Nicole thought. Feeling that there was no way out. He'd helped her think outside the box and see her grandfather's bequest another way: that it could be her escape route. Maybe she could do the same for him.

Could you recruit someone to replace you?

There was a long silence, and Nicole thought maybe she'd gone too far.

Nice idea, Georgy, but it's not going to happen.

OK. What about changing your role in the business instead? Could you take it in a different direction, one you enjoy more?

It's certainly worth thinking about.

Which was a polite brush-off. Just as well she hadn't given in to the urge to suggest meeting for dinner to talk about it.

Because that would've been stupid.

Apart from the fact that she wasn't interested in dating anyone ever again, for all she knew Clarence could be in a serious relationship. Living with someone, engaged, even married.

Even if he wasn't, supposing they met and she discovered that the real Clarence was nothing like the online one? Supposing they really didn't like each other in real life? She valued his friendship too much to risk losing it. If that made her a coward, so be it.

Changing his role in the business. Taking it in a different direction. Gabriel could just imagine the expression on his father's face if he suggested it. Shock, swiftly followed by, 'I saved your skin, so you toe the line and do what I say.'

It wasn't going to happen.

But he appreciated the fact that Georgygirl was trying to think about how to make his life better.

For one mad moment, he almost suggested she should bring details of the business she'd just inherited and meet him for dinner and they could brainstorm it properly. But he stopped himself. Apart from the fact that it was none of his business, supposing they met and he discovered that the real Georgygirl was nothing like the online one? Supposing they loathed each other in real life? He valued his time talking to her and he didn't want to risk losing her friendship.

Thanks for making me feel human again, he typed.

Me? I didn't do anything. And you gave me some really good advice.

That's what friends are for. And you did a lot, believe me. He paused. I'd better let you go. I'm due back in the office. Talk to you later?

I'm due back at the office, too. Talk to you tonight.

Good luck. Let me know how it goes with your mum.

Will do. Let me know how it goes with your family.

Sure.

Though he had no intention of doing that.

CHAPTER TWO

BY THE TIME Nicole went to the restaurant to meet her mother that evening, she had a full dossier on the Electric Palace and its history, thanks to the Surrey Quays forum website. Brian Thomas had owned the cinema since the nineteen-fifties, and it had flourished in the next couple of decades; then it had floundered with the rise of multiplex cinemas and customers demanding something more sophisticated than an old, slightly shabby picture house. One article even described the place as a 'flea-pit'.

Then there were the photographs. It was odd, looking at pictures that people had posted from the nineteen-sixties and realising that the man behind the counter in the café was actually her grandfather, and at the time her mother would've been a toddler. Nicole could definitely see a resemblance to her mother in his face—and to herself. Which made the whole thing feel even more odd. This particular thread was about the history of some of the buildings in Surrey Quays, but it was turning out to be her personal history as well.

Susan hardly ever talked about her family, so Nicole didn't have a clue. Had the Thomas family always lived in Surrey Quays? Had her mother grown up around here? If so, why hadn't she said a word when Nicole had bought her flat, three years ago? Had Nicole spent all this time living only a couple of streets away from the grandparents who'd rejected her?

And how was Susan going to react to the news of the bequest? Would it upset her and bring back bad memories? The last thing Nicole wanted to do was to hurt her mother.

She'd just put the file back in her briefcase when Susan walked over to their table and greeted her with a kiss.

'Hello, darling. I got here as fast as I could. Though it must be serious for you not to be at work at *this* time of day.'

Half-past seven. When most normal people would've left the office hours ago. Nicole grimaced as her mother sat down opposite her. 'Mum. Please.' She really wasn't in the mood for another lecture about her working hours.

'I know, I know. Don't nag. But you do work too hard.' Susan frowned. 'What's happened, love?'

'You know I went to see that solicitor today?'

'Yes.'

'I've been left something in a will.' Nicole blew out a breath. 'I don't think I can accept it.'

'Why not?'

There was no way to say this tactfully. Even though she'd been trying out and discarding different phrases all day, she hadn't found the right words. So all she could do was to come straight out with it. 'Because it's the Electric Palace.'

Understanding dawned in Susan's expression. 'Ah. I did wonder if that would happen.'

Her mother already knew about it? Nicole stared at her in surprise. But how?

As if the questions were written all over her

daughter's face, Susan said gently, 'He had to leave it to someone. You were the obvious choice.'

Nicole shook her head. 'How? Mum, I pass the Electric Palace every day on my way to work. I had no idea it was anything to do with us.'

'It isn't,' Susan said. 'It was Brian's. But I'm glad he's finally done the right thing and left it to you.'

'But you're his daughter, Mum. He should've left it to you, not to me.'

'I don't want it.' Susan lifted her chin. 'Brian made his choice years ago—he decided nearly thirty years ago that I wasn't his daughter and he is most definitely not my father. I don't need anything from him. What I own, I have nobody to thank for but myself. I worked for it. And that's the way I like it.'

Nicole reached over and squeezed her mother's hand. 'And you wonder where I get my stubborn streak?'

Susan gave her a wry smile. 'I guess.'

'I can't accept the bequest,' Nicole said again. 'I'm going to tell the solicitor to make the deeds over to you.'

'Darling, no. Brian left it to you, not to me.'

'But you're his daughter,' Nicole said again.

'And you're his granddaughter,' Susan countered.

Nicole shrugged. 'OK. Maybe I'll sell to the developer who wants it.'

'And you'll use the money to do something that makes you happy?'

It was the perfect answer. 'Yes,' Nicole said. 'Giving the money to you will make me very happy. You can pay off your mortgage and get a new car and go on holiday. It'd be enough for you to go and see the Northern Lights this winter, and I know that's top of your bucket list.'

'Absolutely not.' Susan folded her arms. 'You using that money to get out of that hell-hole you work in would make me much happier than if I spent a single penny on myself, believe me.'

Nicole sighed. 'It feels like blood money, Mum. How can I accept something from someone who behaved so badly to you?'

'Someone who knew he was in the wrong but was too stubborn to apologise. That's where we both get our stubborn streak,' Susan said. 'I think leaving the cinema to you is his way of saying sorry without actually having to use the five-letter word.'

'That's what Cl—' Realising what she was about to give away, Nicole stopped short.

'Cl—?' Susan tipped her head to one side. 'And who might this "Cl—" be?'

'A friend,' Nicole said grudgingly.

'A *male* friend?'

'Yes.' Given that they'd never met in real life, there was always the possibility that her internet friend was actually a woman trying on a male persona for size, but Nicole was pretty sure that Clarence was a man.

'That's good.' Susan looked approving. 'What's his name? Cliff? Clive?'

Uh-oh. Nicole could actually see the match-making gleam in her mother's eye. 'Mum, we're *just* friends.' She didn't want to admit that they'd never actually met and Clarence wasn't even his real name; she knew what conclusion her mother would draw. That Nicole was an utter coward. And there was a lot of truth in that: Nicole was definitely a coward when it came to relationships. She'd been burned badly enough last time to make her very wary indeed.

'You are allowed to date again, you know,' Susan said gently. 'Yes, you picked the wrong one last time—but don't let that put you off. Not all men are as spineless and as selfish as Jeff.'

It was easier to smile and say, 'Sure.' Though Nicole had no intention of dating Clarence. Even if he was available, she didn't want to risk losing his friendship. Wanting to switch the subject away from the abject failure that was her love life, Nicole asked, 'So did you grow up in Surrey Quays, Mum?'

'Back when it was all warehouses and terraced houses, before they were turned into posh flats.' Susan nodded. 'We lived on Mortimer Gardens, a few doors down from the cinema. Those houses were knocked down years ago and the land was redeveloped.'

'Why didn't you say anything when I moved here?'

Susan shrugged. 'You were having a hard enough time. You seemed happy here and you didn't need my baggage weighing you down.'

'So all this time I was living just round the corner from my grandparents? I could've passed them every day in the street without knowing who they were.' The whole thing made her feel uncomfortable.

'Your grandmother died ten years ago,' Susan said. 'When they moved from Mortimer Gardens, they lived at the other end of Surrey Quays from you, so you probably wouldn't have seen Brian, either.'

Which made Nicole feel very slightly better. 'Did you ever work at the cinema?'

'When I was a teenager,' Susan said. 'I was an usherette at first, and then I worked in the ticket office and the café. I filled in and helped with whatever needed doing, really.'

'So you would probably have ended up running the place if you hadn't had me?' Guilt flooded through Nicole. How much her mother had lost in keeping her.

'Having you,' Susan said firmly, 'is the best thing that ever happened to me. The moment I first held you in my arms, I felt this massive rush of love for you and that's never changed. You've brought me more joy over the years than anyone or anything else. And I don't have a single regret about it. I never have and I never will.'

Nicole blinked back the sudden tears. 'I love you, Mum. And I don't mean to bring back bad memories.'

'I love you, too, and you're not bringing back bad memories,' Susan said. 'Now, let's order dinner. And then we'll talk strategy and how you're going to deal with this.'

A plate of pasta and a glass of red wine definitely made Nicole feel more human.

'There's a lot about the cinema on the Surrey Quays website. There's a whole thread with loads of pictures.' Nicole flicked into her phone and showed a few of them to her mother.

'Obviously I was born in the mid-sixties so I don't remember it ever being called The Kursaal,' Susan said, 'but I do remember the place from the seventies on. There was this terrible orange and purple wallpaper in the foyer. You can see it there—just be thankful the photo's black and white.' She smiled. 'I remember queuing with my mum and my friends to see Disney films, and everyone being excited about *Grease*—we were all in love with John Travolta and wanted to look like Sandy and be one of the Pink Ladies. And I remember trying to sneak my friends into *Saturday Night Fever* when we were all too young to get in, and Brian spotting us and marching us into his office, where he yelled at us and said we could lose him his cinema licence.'

'So there were some good times?' Nicole asked.

'There are always good times, if you look for them,' Susan said.

'I remember you taking me to the cinema when I was little,' Nicole said. 'Never to the Electric Palace, though.'

'No, never to the Electric Palace,' Susan said quietly. 'I nearly did—but if Brian and Patsy weren't going to be swayed by the photographs I sent of you on every birthday and Christmas, they probably weren't going to be nice to you if they met you, and I wasn't going to risk them making you cry.'

'Mum, that's so sad.'

'Hey. You have the best godparents ever. And we've got each other. We didn't need them. We're doing just fine, kiddo. And life is too short not to be happy.' Susan put her arm around her.

'I'm fine with my life as it is,' Nicole said.

Susan's expression said very firmly, Like hell you are. But she said, 'You know, it doesn't have to be a cinema.'

'What doesn't?'

'The Electric Palace. It says here on that website that it was a ballroom and an ice rink when it was first built—and you could redevelop it for the twenty-first century.'

'What, turn it back into a ballroom and an ice rink?'

'No. When you were younger, you always liked craft stuff. You could turn it into a craft centre. It would do well around here—people wanting to chill out after work.' Susan gave her a level look. 'People like you who spend too many hours behind a corporate desk and need to do something to help them relax. Look how popular those adult colouring books are—and craft things are even better when they're part of a group thing.'

'A craft centre.' How many years was it since Nicole had painted anything, or sewn anything?

She missed how much she enjoyed being creative, but she never had the time.

'And a café. Or maybe you could try making the old cinema a going concern,' Susan suggested. 'You're used to putting in long hours, but at least this time it'd be for you instead of giving up your whole life to a job you hate.'

Nicole almost said, 'That's what Clarence suggested,' but stopped herself in time. She didn't want her mother knowing that she'd shared that much with him. It would give Susan completely the wrong idea. Nicole wasn't romantically involved with Clarence and didn't intend to be. She wasn't going to be romantically involved with anyone, ever again.

'Think about it,' Susan said. 'Isn't it time you found something that made you happy?'

'I'm perfectly happy in my job,' Nicole lied.

'No, you're not. You hate it, but it makes you financially secure so you'll put up with it—and I know that's my fault because we were so poor when you were little.'

Nicole reached over the table and hugged her. 'Mum, I never felt deprived when I was growing up. You were working three jobs to keep the rent paid and put food on the table, but you always had time for me. Time to give me a cuddle and tell me stories and do a colouring book with me.'

'But you're worried about being poor again. That's why you stick it out.'

'Not so much poor as vulnerable,' Nicole corrected softly. 'My job gives me freedom from that because I don't have to worry if I'm going to be able to pay my mortgage at the end of the month—and that's a good thing. Having a good salary means I have choices. I'm not backed into a corner because of financial constraints.'

'But the hours you put in don't leave you time for anything else. You don't do anything for *you*—and maybe that's what the Electric Palace can do for you.'

Nicole doubted that very much, but wanted to avoid a row. 'Maybe.'

'Did the solicitor give you the keys?'

Nicole nodded. 'Shall we go and look at it, then have coffee and pudding back at my place?'

'Great idea,' Susan said.

The place was boarded up; all they could see of

the building was the semi-circle on the top of the façade at the front and the pillars on either side of the front door. Nicole wasn't that surprised when the lights didn't work—the electricity supply had probably been switched off—but she kept a mini torch on her key-ring, and the beam was bright enough to show them the inside of the building.

Susan sniffed. 'Musty. But no damp, hopefully.'

'What's that other smell?' Nicole asked, noting the unpleasant acridness.

'I think it might be mice.'

Susan's suspicions were confirmed when they went into the auditorium and saw how many of the plush seats looked nibbled. Those that had escaped the mice's teeth were worn threadbare in places.

'I can see why that article called it a flea-pit,' Nicole said with a shudder. 'This is awful, Mum.'

'You just need the pest control people in for the mice, then do a bit of scrubbing,' Susan said.

But when they came out of the auditorium and back into the foyer, Nicole flashed the torch around and saw the stained glass. 'Oh, Mum, that's gorgeous. And the wood on the bar—it's pitted in places, but I bet a carpenter could sort that out. I can just see this bar restored to its Edwardian Art Deco glory.'

'Back in its earliest days?' Susan asked.

'Maybe. And look at this staircase.' Nicole shone the torch on the sweeping wrought-iron staircase that led up to the first floor. 'I can imagine movie stars sashaying down this in high heels and gorgeous dresses. Or glamorous ballroom dancers.'

'We never really used the upper floor. There was always a rope across the stairs,' Susan said.

'So what's upstairs?'

Susan shrugged. 'Brian's office was there. As for the rest of it… Storage space, I think.'

But when they went to look, they discovered that the large upstairs room had gorgeous parquet flooring, and a ceiling covered in carved Art Deco stars that stunned them both.

'I had no idea this was here,' Susan said. 'How beautiful.'

'This must've been the ballroom bit,' Nicole said. 'And I can imagine people dancing here during the Blitz, refusing to let the war get them down. Mum, this place is incredible.'

She'd never expected to fall in love with a building, especially one which came from a source that made her feel awkward and uncomfortable. But Nicole could see the Electric Palace as it could be if it was renovated—the cinema on the ground floor, with the top floor as a ballroom or maybe a place for local bands to play. Or she could even turn this room into a café-restaurant. A café with an area for doing crafts, perhaps like her mum suggested. Or an ice cream parlour, stocked with local artisan ice cream.

If she just sold the Electric Palace to a developer and collected the money, would the building be razed to the ground? Could all this be lost?

But she really couldn't let that happen. She wanted to bring the Electric Palace back to life, to make it part of the community again.

'It's going to be a lot of work to restore it,' she said. Not to mention money: it would eat up all her savings and she would probably need a bank loan as well to tide her over until the business was up and running properly.

'But you're not afraid of hard work—and this time you'd be working for you,' Susan pointed out.

'On the Surrey Quays forum, quite a few people have said how they'd love the place to be restored so we had our own cinema locally,' Nicole said thoughtfully.

'So you wouldn't be doing it on your own,' Susan said. 'You already have a potential audience and people who'd be willing to spread the word. Some of them might volunteer to help you with the restoration or running the place—and you can count me in as well. I could even try and get some of my probationers interested. I bet they'd enjoy slapping a bit of paint on the walls.'

'Supposing I can't make a go of it? There's only one screen, maybe the possibility of two if I use the upstairs room,' Nicole said. 'Is that enough to draw the customers in and make the place pay?'

'If anyone can do it, you can,' Susan said.

'I have savings,' Nicole said thoughtfully. 'If the renovations cost more than what I have, I could get a loan.'

'I have savings, too. I'd be happy to use them here,' Susan added.

Nicole shook her head. 'This should be your heritage, Mum, not mine. And I don't want you to risk your savings on a business venture that might not make it.'

'We've already had this argument. You didn't win it earlier and you're not going to win it now,' Susan said crisply. 'The Electric Palace is yours. And it's your choice whether you want to sell it or whether you want to do something with it.'

Nicole looked at the sad, neglected old building and knew exactly what she was going to do. 'I'll work out some figures, to see if it's viable.' Though she knew that it wasn't just about the figures. And if the figures didn't work, she'd find alternatives until they *did* work.

'And if it's viable?' Susan asked.

'I'll talk to my boss. If he'll give me a six-month sabbatical, it'd be long enough for me to see if I can make a go of this place.' Nicole shook her head. 'I can't quite believe I just said that. I've spent ten years working for the bank and I've worked my way up from the bottom.'

'And you hate it there—it suppresses the real Nicole and it's turned you into a corporate ghost.'

'Don't pull your punches, Mum,' Nicole said wryly.

Susan hugged her. 'I can love you to bits at the same time as telling you that you're making a massive mistake with your life, you know.'

'Because mums are good at multi-tasking?'

'You got it, kiddo.' Susan hugged her again. 'And I'm with you on this. Anything you need, from scrubbing floors to working a shift in the ticket office to making popcorn, I'm there—and, as I said, I have savings and I'm happy to invest them in this place.'

'You worked hard for that money.'

'And interest rates are so pathetic that my savings are earning me nothing. I'd rather that money was put to good use. Making my daughter's life better—and that would make me very happy indeed. You can't put a price on that.'

Nicole hugged her. 'Thanks, Mum. I love you. And you are so getting the best pudding in the world.'

'You mean, we have to stop by the supermarket on the way back to your flat because there's nothing in your fridge,' Susan said dryly.

Nicole grinned. 'You know me so well.'

Later that evening, when Susan had gone home, Nicole checked her phone. As she'd half expected, there was a message from Clarence. Did you talk to your mum?

Yes. Did you talk to your dad?

To her pleasure, he replied almost instantly.

No. There wasn't time.

Nicole was pretty sure that meant Clarence hadn't been able to face a row.

What did your mum say? he asked.

Even though she had a feeling that he was asking her partly to distract her from quizzing him about his own situation, it was still nice that he was interested.

We went to see the building.

And?

It's gorgeous but it needs work.

Then I'd recommend getting a full surveyor's report, so you can make sure any renovation quotes you get from builders are fair, accurate and complete.

Thanks. I hadn't thought of that.

I can recommend some people, if you want.

That'd be great. I'll take you up on that, if the figures stack up and I decide to go ahead with getting the business back up and running.

Although Nicole had told herself she'd only do it if the figures worked out, she knew it was a fib. She'd fallen in love with the building and for the first time in years she was excited at the idea of starting work on something. Clarence obviously lived in Surrey Quays, or he wouldn't be part of the forum; so he'd see the boards come down from the front of the Electric Palace or hear about the renovations from some other eagle-eyed person on the Surrey Quays website.

She really ought to tell him before it started happening. After all, he was her friend. And he'd said that he had experience in the entertainment and service industry, so he might have some great ideas for getting the cinema up and running again. He'd already made her think about having a survey done, which wouldn't have occurred to her—she'd just intended to find three builders with good reputations and would pick the middle quote of the three.

But, even as she started to type her news, something held her back.

And she knew what it was. Jeff's betrayal had broken her trust. Although she felt she knew Clarence well, and he was the only person she'd even consider talking to about this apart from her mum and best friend, she found herself halting instead of typing a flurry of excited words about her plans.

Maybe it was better to wait to tell him about it until she'd got all her ducks in a row and knew exactly what she was doing.

What's stopping you going ahead? he asked.

I need to work out the figures first. See if it's viable.

So your mum said the same as I did—that it'll get you out of the job you hate?

Yes, she admitted.

Good—and you're listening to both of us?

I'm listening, she said. But it's still early days, Clarence. I don't want to talk about it too much right now—

She couldn't tell him that she didn't trust him. That would mean explaining about Jeff, and she still cringed when she thought about it. How she'd been blithely unaware of the real reason Jeff had asked her to live with him, until she'd overheard that conversation in the toilets. One of the women touching up her make-up by the mirror had said how her boyfriend was actually living with someone else right then but didn't love her—he was only living with the other woman because his boss wasn't prepared to give the promotion to someone who wasn't settled down, and he was going to leave her as soon as he got the promotion.

Nicole had winced in sympathy with the poor, deluded woman who thought everything was fine, and also wanted to point out to the woman bragging about her fickle lover that, if he was prepared to cheat on his live-in girlfriend with her, there was a very strong chance he'd do exactly the same thing to her with someone else at some point in the future.

The woman had continued, 'She's a right cold fish, Jeff says. A boring banker. But Jeff says he really, really loves me. He's even bought me an engagement ring—look.'

There were encouraging coos from her friends; but Nicole had found herself going cold. Jeff wasn't exactly a common name. Even if it were how many men called Jeff were living with a girlfriend who was a banker? Surely it couldn't be…? But when the woman had gone on to describe cheating, lying Jeff, Nicole had realised with devastating clarity that the poor, deluded woman she'd felt sorry for was none other than herself.

She shook herself. That was all baggage that she needed to jettison. And right now Clarence was waiting for her reply.

She continued typing.

In case I jinx it. The building's going to need a lot of work doing to it. I don't mean to be offensive and shut you out.

It is what it is, he said. No offence taken. And when you do want to talk about it, Georgy, I'm here.

I know, Clarence. And I appreciate it.

She appreciated the fact he kept things light in the rest of their conversation, too.

Goodnight, Georgy. Sweet dreams.

You, too, Clarence.

CHAPTER THREE

'IT'S A PIPE DREAM, Gabriel. You can't create something out of nothing. We're not going to be able to offer our guests exclusive parking.' Evan Hunter stared at his son. 'We should've got the land on the other side of the hotel.'

'It was a sealed bid auction, Dad. And we agreed what would be reasonable. Paying over the odds for the land would've wrecked our budget and the hotel might not have been viable any more.'

'And in the meantime there's an apartment block planned for where our car park should be,' Evan grumbled.

'Unless the new owner of the Electric Palace sells to us.'

Evan sighed. 'Nicole Thomas has already turned

down every offer. She says she's going to restore the place.'

'It might not be worth her while,' Gabriel pointed out. 'She's a banker. She'll understand about gearing—and if the restoration costs are too high, she'll see the sense in selling.' He paused. 'To us.'

'You won't succeed, Gabriel. It's a waste of time.'

Maybe, Gabriel thought, this was his chance to prove his worth to his father once and for all. 'I'll talk to her.'

'Charm her into it?' Evan scoffed.

'Give her a dose of healthy realism,' Gabriel corrected. 'The place has been boarded up for five years. The paintwork outside is in bad condition. There are articles in the Surrey Quays forum from years back calling it a flea-pit, so my guess is that it's even worse inside. Add damp, mould and vermin damage—it's not going to be cheap to fix that kind of damage.'

'The Surrey Quays forum.' Evan's eyes narrowed. 'If she gets them behind her and starts a pressure group…'

'Dad. I'll handle it,' Gabriel said. 'We haven't had any objections to the hotel, have we?'

'I suppose not.'

Gabriel didn't bother waiting for his father to say he'd done a good job with the PR side. It wasn't Evan's style. 'I'll handle it,' he said again. 'Nicole Thomas is a hard-headed businesswoman. She'll see the sensible course is to sell the site to us. She gets to cash in her inheritance, and we get the space. Everybody wins.'

'Hmm.' Evan didn't look convinced.

So maybe this would be the tipping point. The thing that finally earned Gabriel his father's respect.

And then maybe he'd get his freedom.

The figures worked. So did the admin. Nicole had checked online and there was a huge list of permissions and licences she needed to apply for, but it was all doable. She just needed to make a master list, do some critical path analysis, and tackle the tasks in the right order. Just as she would on a normal day at her desk.

Once she'd talked to her boss and he'd agreed

to let her take a sabbatical, she sat at her desk, working out how to break the news to her team.

But then Neil, her second-in-command, came in to her office. 'Are the rumours true?'

It looked as if the office grapevine had scooped her. 'What rumours?' she asked, playing for time.

'That you're taking six months off?'

'Yes.'

He looked her up and down, frowning. 'You don't *look* pregnant.'

Oh, honestly. Was the guy still stuck in the Dark Ages? 'That's because I'm not.'

'Then what? Have you got yourself a mail-order bridegroom on the internet—a rich Russian mafia guy who wants to be respectable?' He cackled, clearly pleased with himself at the barb.

She rolled her eyes, not rising to the bait. Neil liked to think of himself as the office wise-guy and he invariably made comments for a cheap laugh at other people's expense. She'd warned him about it before in his annual review, but he hadn't taken a blind bit of notice. 'You can tell everyone I'm not pregnant. I'm also not running off to Russia, thinking that I've bagged myself a millionaire bridegroom only to discover that it was all a big scam and I'm about to be sold into slavery.' She steepled her fingers and looked him straight in the eye. 'Are there any other rumours I need to clarify, or are we done?'

'Wow—I've never heard you…' He looked at her with something akin to respect. 'Sorry.'

She shrugged. 'Apology accepted.'

'So why are you taking six months off?'

'It's a business opportunity,' she said. 'Keep your fingers crossed that it works, because if it doesn't I'll be claiming my desk back in six months' time.'

From him, she meant, and clearly he recognised it because his face went dull red. 'No offence meant.'

'Good,' she said, and clapped him on the shoulder. 'Little tip from me. For what's probably the six millionth time I've told you, Neil, try to lose the wisecracks. They make you look less professional and that'll stand in the way of you being promoted.'

'All right. Sorry.' He paused. 'Are you really going today?'

'Yes.'

'Without even having a leaving do?'

'I might be coming back if my plans don't work out,' she reminded him, 'so it would be a bit fake to have a leaving do. But I'll put some money behind the bar at the Mucky Duck—' the nearby pub that most of her team seemed to frequent after work '—if you're all that desperate to have a drink at my expense.'

'Hang on. You'll pay for your own sort-of leaving do and not turn up to it?'

That was the idea. She spread her hands. 'What's the problem?'

Neil shook his head. 'If it wasn't for the fact you're actually leaving, I'd think you'd be slaving behind your desk. You never join in with anything.'

'Because I don't fit in,' she said softly. 'So I'm not going to be the spectre at the feast. You can all enjoy a drink without worrying what to say in front of me.'

'None of us really knows you—all we know is that you work crazy hours,' Neil said.

Which was why nobody ever asked her about

how her weekend was: they knew she would've spent a big chunk of Saturday at her desk.

'Do you even have a life outside the office?' Neil asked.

And this time there was no barb in his voice; Nicole squirmed inwardly when she realised that the odd note in his voice was pity. 'Ask me again in six months,' she said, 'because then I hope I might have.' And that was the nearest she'd get to admitting her work-life balance was all wrong.

'Well—good luck with your mysterious business opportunity,' he said.

'Thanks—and I'll make sure I leave my desk tidy for you.'

Neil took it as the dismissal she meant it to be; but, before she could clear her desk at the end of the day, her entire team filed into her office, headed by her boss.

'We thought you should have these,' he said, and presented her with a bottle of expensive champagne, a massive card which had been signed by everyone on their floor, and a huge bouquet of roses and lilies.

'We didn't really know what to get you,' Neil

said, joining them at Nicole's desk, 'but the team had a whip-round.' He presented her with an envelope filled with money. 'Maybe this will help with your, um, business opportunity.'

Nicole was touched that they'd gone to this trouble. She hadn't expected anything—just that she'd slip away quietly while everyone else was at the bar across the road.

'Thanks. You'll be pleased to know it'll go to good use—I'll probably spend it on paint.'

Neil gaped at her. 'You're leaving us to be an artist?'

She laughed. 'No. I meant masonry paint. I've been left a cinema in a will. It's a bit run-down but I'm going to restore it and see if I can get it up and running properly.'

'A *cinema*? Then you,' Neil said, 'are coming across to the Mucky Duck with us right now, and you're going to tell us everything—and that's not a suggestion, Nicole, because we'll carry you over there if we have to.'

It was the first time Nicole had actually felt part of the team. How ironic that it had happened just as she was leaving them.

'OK,' she said, and let them sweep her across the road in the middle of a crowd.

The next day, Nicole was in the cinema with a clipboard and a pen, adding to her list of what she needed to do when her phone rang.

She glanced at the screen, half expecting that it would be her daily call from the lawyer at Hunter Hotels trying to persuade her to sell the Electric Palace, even though she'd told him every time that the cinema wasn't for sale. Not recognising the number on her screen, and assuming it was one of the calls she was waiting to be returned, she answered her phone. 'Yes?'

'Ms Thomas?'

'Yes.'

'It's Gabriel Hunter from Hunter Hotels.'

Clearly the lawyer had realised that she wasn't going to say yes to the monkey, so now it was the organ-grinder's turn to try and persuade her. She suppressed a sigh. 'Thank you for calling, Mr Hunter, but I believe I've made my position quite clear. The Electric Palace isn't for sale.'

'Indeed,' he said, 'but we have areas of mutual interest and I'd like to meet you to discuss them.'

In other words, he planned to charm her into selling? She put on her best bland voice. 'That's very nice of you to ask, but I'm afraid I'm really rather busy at the moment.'

'It won't take long. Are you at the cinema right now?'

'Yes.'

She regretted her answer the moment he asked, 'And you've been there since the crack of dawn?'

Had the Hunters got someone spying on her, or something? 'Not that it's any of your business, but yes.' There was a lot to do. And she thought at her best, first thing in the morning. It made sense to start early.

'I'd be the same,' he said, mollifying her only slightly. 'So I'd say you're about due for a coffee break. How about I meet you at the café on Challoner Road in half an hour?'

'Where you'll have a carnation in your buttonhole and be carrying a copy of the *Financial Times* so I can recognise you?' She couldn't help the snippy retort.

He laughed. 'No need. I'll be there first—and I'll recognise you.'

Hunter Hotels probably had a dossier on her, including a photograph and a list of everything from her route to work to her shoe size, she thought grimly. 'Thank you for the invitation, but there really isn't any point in us meeting. I'm not selling.'

'I'm not trying to pressure you to sell. As I said, I want to discuss mutual opportunities—and the coffee's on me.'

'I'm not dressed to go to a café. I'm covered in dust.'

'I'd be worried if you weren't, given the current condition of the cinema. And I'd be even more worried if you were walking around a run-down building wearing patent stilettos and a business suit.'

There was a note of humour in Gabriel Hunter's voice. Nicole hadn't expected that, and she quite liked it; at the same time, it left her feeling slightly off balance.

'But if you'd rather I brought the coffee to you, that's fine,' he said. 'Just let me know how you take your coffee.'

It was tempting, but at least if they met in a neutral place she could make an excuse to leave. If he turned up at the cinema, she might have to be rude in order to make him leave and let her get on with things. And, at the end of the day, Gabriel Hunter was working on the business next door to hers. They might have mutual customers. So he probably had a point about mutual opportunities. Maybe they should talk.

'I'll see you at the café in half an hour,' she said.

She brushed herself down and then was cross with herself. It wasn't as if he was her client, and she wasn't still working at the bank. It didn't matter what she looked like or what he thought of her. And if he tried to push her into selling the Electric Palace, she'd give him very short shrift and come back to work on her lists.

So Nicole Thomas had agreed to meet him. That was a good start, Gabriel thought. He'd certainly got further with her than their company lawyer had.

He worked on his laptop with one eye on the

door, waiting for her to turn up. Given that she'd worked in a bank and her photograph on their website made her look like a consummate professional, he'd bet that she'd walk through the door thirty seconds earlier than they'd agreed to meet. Efficiency was probably her middle name.

Almost on cue, the door opened. He recognised Nicole immediately; even though she was wearing old jeans and a T-shirt rather than a business suit, and no make-up whatsoever, her mid-brown hair was pulled back in exactly the same style as she'd worn it at the bank. Old habits clearly died hard.

She glanced around the café, obviously looking for him. For a moment, she looked vulnerable and Gabriel was shocked to feel a sudden surge of protectiveness. She worked for a bank and had worked her way up the management ladder, so she most definitely didn't need protecting; but there was something about her that drew him.

He was horrified to realise that he was attracted to her.

Talk about inappropriate. You didn't fall for

your business rival. Ever. Besides, he didn't want to get involved with anyone. He was tired of dating women who had preconceived notions about him. All he wanted to do was talk to Nicole Thomas about mutual opportunities, point out all the many difficulties she was going to face in restoring the cinema, and then talk her into doing the sensible thing and selling the Electric Palace to him for a price fair to both of them.

Nicole looked round the café, trying to work out which of the men sitting on their own was Gabriel Hunter. Why on earth hadn't she looked him up on the internet first, so she would've known exactly who she was meeting here? Had she already slipped out of good business habits, just days after leaving the bank? At this rate, she'd make a complete mess of the cinema and she'd be forced to go back to her old job—and, worse still, have to admit that she'd failed in her bid for freedom.

Then the man in the corner lifted his hand and gave the tiniest wave.

He looked young—probably around her own

age. There wasn't a hint of grey in his short dark hair, and his blue eyes were piercing.

If he was the head of Hunter Hotels when he was that young, then he was definitely the ruthless kind. She made a mental note to be polite but to stay on her guard.

His suit was expensively cut—the sort that had been hand-made by a good tailor, rather than bought off the peg—and she'd just bet if she looked under the table his shoes would be the same kind of quality. His shirt was well cut, too, and that understated tie was top of the range. He radiated money and style, looking more like a model advertising a super-expensive watch than a hotel magnate, and she felt totally scruffy and underdressed in her jeans and T-shirt. Right then she really missed the armour of her business suit.

He stood up as she reached his table and held out his hand. 'Thank you for coming, Ms Thomas.'

His handshake was firm and a little tingle ran down Nicole's spine at the touch of his skin against hers. How inappropriate was that? They were on opposite sides and she'd better remember that. Apart from the fact that she never wanted to get involved with anyone again, the fact Gabriel Hunter was her business rival meant he was totally out of the running as a potential date. Even if he was one of the nicest-looking men she'd ever met. Didn't they say that handsome is as handsome does?

'Mr Hunter,' she said coolly.

'Call me Gabriel.'

She had no intention of doing that—or of inviting him to call her by her own first name. They weren't friends; they were business rivals.

'How do you like your coffee?' he asked.

'Espresso, please.'

'Me, too.' He smiled at her, and her heart felt as if it had done a backflip.

'If you haven't been here before, I'd recommend the Guatemala blend.'

'Thank you. That would be lovely,' she said politely.

This was the kind of café that sold a dozen different types of coffee, from simple Americanos and cappuccinos through to pour-over-and-siphon coffee; and she noted from the chalk board above the counter that there were a dozen different blends to choose from, all with tasting notes, so this was the kind of place that was frequented by serious coffee drinkers. The kind of coffee bar she half had in mind for the Electric Palace, depending on whether she kept it as a cinema or turned it into a craft café.

But Gabriel Hunter unsettled her.

She wasn't used to reacting like that towards someone. She hadn't reacted to anyone like that since Jeff. Given her poor judgement when it came to relationships, she really didn't want to be attracted to Gabriel Hunter.

Focus, Nicole, she told herself sharply. Business. Work. Nothing else.

Gabriel came back to the table carrying two espressos, and set one cup and saucer in front of her before sitting down opposite her again.

She took a sip. 'You're right; this is excellent. Thank you.'

'Pleasure.' He inclined his head.

Enough pleasantries, she decided. This was business, so they might as well save some time and cut to the chase. 'So, what are these mutual interests you wanted to discuss?' she asked.

'Our businesses are next door to each other. And they're both works in progress,' he said, 'though obviously the hotel renovation is quite a bit further on than the cinema.'

'Are you thinking mutual customers?'

'And mutual parking.'

His eyes really were sharp, she thought. As if they saw everything.

'Are you really going to run the place as a cinema?' he asked.

She frowned. 'Why would I discuss my business strategy with a competitor?'

'True. But, if you are going to run it as a cinema, I'm not sure you'll manage to make it pay, and it's not going to be good for my business if the place next door to me is boarded up and looks derelict,' he said bluntly. 'Most people would choose to take the Tube into the West End and go to a multiplex to see the latest blockbuster. One screen doesn't give your customers a lot of choice, and you'll be competing directly with established businesses that can offer those customers an awful lot more.'

'That all depends on the programming.' She'd been researching that; and she needed to think about whether to show the blockbusters as they came out, or to develop the Electric Palace as an art-house cinema, or to have a diverse programme with certain kinds of movies showing on certain nights.

'With your background in banking—' well, of course he'd checked her out and would know that '—obviously you're more than capable of handling the figures and the finance,' he said. 'But the building needs a lot of work, and restoring something properly takes a lot of experience or at least knowing who to ask.'

'It's been boarded up for the last five years. How would you know the place needs a lot of work?' she asked.

'Because if you leave any building without any kind of maintenance for five years, there's going to be a problem,' he said matter-of-factly. 'Anything from damp caused by the tiniest leak in the roof that's built up unnoticed over the years, through to damage from mice or rats. None of it will be covered by insurance—assuming that there was any premises insurance in place at all while it was closed—because that kind of damage counts as a gradually operating cause.'

There was definitely insurance in place. That was the first thing she'd checked. But she also knew he had a point about uninsured damage. And she'd noticed that he was using legal terms as if he was very, very familiar with even the tiniest of small print. She'd need to be very careful how she dealt with him.

'And then there's the state of the wiring and the plumbing,' he continued. 'Even if the rats and mice have left it alone, the cabling's probably deteriorated with age, and do you even know when it was last rewired? For all you know, it could still be nineteen-fifties wiring and it'd need replacing completely to make it safe. Without safe wiring, you won't get public liability insurance or any of the business licences you need.'

Just when she thought he'd finished, he continued, 'And then there's lead piping. Unless your water pipes have been completely replaced since the nineteen-sixties, there's a good chance you'll have lead piping. You'll need to get that replaced—just as we're having to do, next door.'

She didn't have a clue when the wiring had last been done, or even how to check what its current state was like, or how to check the water pipes. 'That's precisely why I'm having a survey done,' she said, grateful that Clarence had suggested that to her. 'So then I'll know exactly what needs to be done and what to ask builders to quote for.'

'So where are your customers going to park?' he asked.

'The same place as they would at the multiplexes in town—there's no need to park, because they'll either walk here or take the Tube,' she countered. 'Where are yours going to park?'

Even though he was pretty impassive, there was the tiniest flicker in his eyes that gave him away. And then she realised. 'That's why you want to buy the Electric Palace,' she said. 'So you can raze it to the ground and turn the space into a car park.'

'It's one option.' He shrugged. 'But if the building is in better condition than I think it is, it could also work as the hotel's restaurant or conference suite.'

She shook her head. 'It's not a restaurant. It's a purpose-built cinema.'

'But it's not a listed building. The use could be changed very easily.'

She stared at him. 'You've already checked that out?'

'As we do with any building we consider developing,' he said, not looking in the slightest bit abashed. 'If a building's listed, it means we'll have to meet strict criteria before we can make any alterations, and it also means extra site visits and inspections—all of which adds time to a project. And time is money.'

She blinked. 'Are you saying you rush things through?'

'No. Cutting corners means offering our clients a substandard experience, and we don't do that. Hunter Hotels is about high quality,' he said. 'What I mean is that if a building isn't listed, then we don't get the extra admin hassle when we renovate it and we don't have any enforced downtime while we wait for inspections.' He looked her straight in the eye. 'Then again, if the council were to decide your cinema ought to be listed…'

'Are you threatening me?'

'No, I'm pointing out that you need to get various licences. The council might look at your application and decide that a purpose-built Edwardian *kursaal* really ought to be on the Statutory List of Buildings of Special Architectural or Historical Interest. Especially as there aren't many of them left.'

His voice was bland, but she was pretty sure he was enjoying this. Gabriel Hunter was a corporate shark—and he'd just spotted a weakness and was playing on it. She narrowed her eyes at him. 'It feels as if you're threatening me.'

'Not at all. I'm just warning you to be prepared, because you clearly don't have any experience of dealing with premises—and, as your building's been boarded up for the last five years, there's a pretty good chance you have hidden damage that's going to take a lot of time and money to sort out. The longer it takes to get the building up and running, the longer it'll be before it starts to pay for itself, and the more likely it is that you'll run into other roadblocks.'

Gabriel Hunter was being perfectly polite and charming, but Nicole thought that he was definitely trying to worry her to the point where she'd think that the burden of restoring the cinema would be too heavy and it would be easier to sell the place. To him. 'The Electric Palace isn't for sale,' she repeated. 'So, unless you have some constructive suggestions—like offering my clients a special pre-movie dinner menu—then I really don't think we have anything more to talk about, Mr Hunter.'

'A special dinner menu is a possibility. And in return you could offer my clients a special deal on ticket prices.'

'You seriously think we could work together?' And yet she couldn't shake the suspicion that this was all a smokescreen. She knew that Hunter Hotels wanted her to sell. 'I've just refused to sell my cinema to you. Why would you want to work with me?'

'It is what it is,' he said.

She looked at him in surprise. 'Clarence says

that all the time.' The words were out before she could stop them.

'Who's Clarence?' he asked.

She shook her head. 'Nobody you know.' Clarence had nothing in common with Gabriel Hunter, and it was extremely unlikely that they knew each other. Even if they did know each other, in real life, they were so different that they probably loathed each other.

Clarence.

It wasn't exactly a common name. Gabriel didn't know anyone else called Clarence, whether in real life or online.

Surely Nicole couldn't be…?

But, as he thought about it, the pieces fell rapidly into place. Georgygirl had just inherited a commercial building—a business she'd been mysterious about. He knew she hated her job, and was planning to take a sabbatical to see if she could turn the business around and make it work.

Nicole Thomas had just inherited the Electric Palace and, according to his sources, she was taking a sabbatical from the bank.

So was Nicole Thomas *Georgygirl*?

This was the first time he'd actually connected his online and real life, and as the penny dropped it left him reeling.

The girl he'd met online was warm and sweet and funny, whereas Nicole Thomas was cool and hard-headed. Georgygirl was his friend, whereas Nicole Thomas had made it very clear that not only were they not friends, they were on opposite sides.

The whole reason he'd resisted meeting Georgygirl was because he'd been afraid that they'd be different in real life, not meeting each other's expectations. And then he'd lose her friendship, a relationship he'd really come to value over the months.

It looked as if his fears had been right on the nail. Georgygirl was completely different in real life. They weren't compatible at all.

Nicole clearly hadn't worked out yet that he was Clarence. Even if she'd researched Hunter Hotels, she wouldn't have connected Clarence with Gabriel. He'd let it slip that he worked in the leisure industry, but that was such a broad category that it was unlikely she'd connect it with hotel development.

Given that they didn't like each other—he ignored that spark of attraction he'd felt, and that surge of protectiveness he'd felt towards her—maybe he could leverage the ruins of their friendship. He could keep pointing out the downsides of the building and the difficulties she was going to face; then he could offer her an easy option. One he hoped she'd take, and she'd sell the Electric Palace to him.

OK, so he'd lose Georgygirl's friendship completely. But he'd pretty much lost that anyway, hadn't he? Once she knew who he was, she'd turn away from him. He'd be naive to think it could be different and could ever lead to anything else.

'I guess you're right,' he said. 'We probably don't have mutual interests. I'll let you get on. Thank you for your time.'

'Thank you for the coffee,' she said.

He gave her the briefest of nods and walked out before his disappointment could betray him.

* * *

Later that evening, a message came in on Gabriel's screen.

Hey, Clarence. How was your day?

OK, I guess, he typed back, feeling slightly uneasy because he knew exactly who she was, while he was pretty sure she still didn't know the truth about him. How was yours?

Pretty grim. I met the guy who wants to buy my business.

Uh-oh. Clarence would be sympathetic; Gabriel wasn't so sure he wanted to hear what she had to say about him.

OK…he said, playing for time.

He's a corporate shark in a suit, she said.

Ouch. Well, it was his own fault. He should've told her face to face who he was when he'd had the chance. Now it was going to get messy. He'd limit the damage and tell her right now.

I had a meeting today too, he said. With someone I was expecting to be my enemy, but who turned out to be someone I've been friends with for a long time.

That's good, isn't it? she asked.

He wasn't so sure. But he was going to have to bite the bullet.

Nicole, I think we need to talk.

Nicole stared at her screen. She'd never, ever given Clarence her real name. So why was he using it now? How did he know who she was?

Then a seriously nasty thought hit her.

She dismissed it instantly. Of course Clarence couldn't be Gabriel Hunter. He just couldn't. Clarence was kind and sweet and funny.

But he knew her real name without her telling him. And there was no way he could have connected Georgygirl with Nicole Thomas. They'd never shared real names or the kind of personal details that would link up. So the only logical explanation was that Clarence was Gabriel.

Are you trying to tell me *you're* the corporate shark? she typed, desperately wanting him to tell her that he wasn't.

But his reply was very clear.

I don't think of myself that way, but you clearly do. Yes. I'm Gabriel Hunter.

Clarence really was Gabriel Hunter?

She couldn't quite take it in.

And then she felt sick to her stomach. Yet again, she'd fallen for someone and he'd turned out to be using her. Jeff had only asked her to date him and then move in with him because he'd wanted promotion and his boss had a thing about only promoting young men if they were settled. And now Clarence had betrayed her in exactly the same way: he hadn't made friends with her because he liked her, but because he'd wanted to leverage their friendship and persuade her to sell the Electric Palace to Hunter Hotels.

What a stupid, naive fool she was.

How long have you known who I am? she demanded, wanting to know the worst so she could regroup.

I only realised today, he said. When you talked about Clarence. Then the pieces fitted together.

You'd inherited a business and you were taking a sabbatical to see if you could make it work. So had Georgy.

But you didn't say a word to me at the café.

I might have got the wrong end of the stick. There might've been another Clarence.

Because it's *such* a common name? she asked waspishly.

OK. I wanted time to get my head round it, he said. Right then I didn't know what to say to you.

So how long have you known that the Electric Palace was mine?

We knew it belonged to Brian Thomas—we'd approached him several times over the last couple of years and he'd refused to sell. We didn't know who his heir was until his will was made public. Then we contacted you—and at that point I didn't know you were Georgy.

He really expected her to believe that?

But now it's out in the open, he continued.

And how.

There's something I'd like you to think about.

Against her better instincts, she asked, What?

You know that art café you talked to me about, a couple of months ago? If you sell the cinema, that'd give you the money to find the perfect place for it. To find a building you're not going to have to restore first. It'll save you so much time and hassle. It'd give you the space to follow your dreams straight away instead of having to wait while you rebuild someone else's.

Nicole stared at the screen in disbelief. He was picking up on the private dream she'd told him about in a completely different context and was using it to pressure her into selling?

You actually think you can use our former friendship to make me sell to you? she asked, not sure whether she was more hurt or disgusted. Oh, please. You're a corporate shark through and through. The Electric Palace isn't for sale—not now and not in the foreseeable future. Goodbye, Clarence.

She flicked out of the messaging programme and shut down her laptop before he could reply.

It was hard to get her head round this. Her friend Clarence was actually her business rival, Gabriel Hunter. Which meant he wasn't really her friend—otherwise why would he have tried to use their relationship to put pressure on her to sell?

And to think she'd told him things she'd never told anyone else. Trusted him.

Now she knew who he really was, her worst fears had come true. He wasn't the same online as he was in real life. In real life, she disliked him and everything he stood for.

She'd lost her friend.

And she'd lost the tiny bit of her remaining trust along with that friendship.

CHAPTER FOUR

GABRIEL'S MOOD THE next day wasn't improved by another run-in with his father—especially because this time he couldn't talk to Georgygirl about it and there was nobody to tease him out of his irritation.

He also couldn't share the bad pun that a friend emailed him and that he knew Georgy would've enjoyed. He thought about sending her a message, but she'd made it pretty clear that she didn't want to have anything to do with him. That 'Goodbye, Clarence' had sounded very final.

She didn't message him that evening, either.

Not that he was surprised. Nicole Thomas wasn't the kind of woman who backed down. She was a cool, hard-headed businesswoman.

By the following morning, Gabriel realised why his dark mood refused to lift. He *missed*

Georgygirl. She'd made his life so much brighter, these last six months. It had felt good, knowing that there was someone out there who actually understood who he really was, at heart. And he was miserable without her.

Did she miss Clarence, too? he wondered.

OK, so Nicole had called him a corporate shark. Which he wasn't. Not really. He wasn't a push-over, but he was scrupulously fair in his business dealings. His real identity had clearly come as a shock to her. Hers had been a shock to him, too, but at least he'd had time to get his head round it before he'd talked to her, whereas he hadn't given her a chance to get used to the idea. Then she'd accused him of using their former friend-ship to make her sell the cinema to him, and he knew she had a point. He *had* tried to leverage their former friendship, thinking that it was all that was left.

But if she missed him as much as he missed her, and she could put aside who he was and see past that to his real self—the self he'd shared with her online—then maybe they could salvage something from this.

In any case, their businesses were next door to each other. It would be the neighbourly thing to do, to take her a coffee and see how she was getting on. The fact that he was attracted to her had nothing to do with it, he told himself. This was strictly business, and maybe also a chance to fix a relationship that he valued and he missed.

He dropped in to his favourite coffee shop—the one where he'd met Nicole the other day—picked up two espressos to go and two dark chocolate brownies, then headed for Mortimer Gardens.

The front door to the cinema was closed, but when he tried the handle it was unlocked. He opened it and went into the lobby. 'Hello?' he called.

Nicole came into the lobby from what he assumed was the foyer, carrying a clipboard. 'What are you doing here?' she asked.

'I brought you coffee.' He offered her the paper cup and one of the two paper bags.

She frowned. 'Why?'

'Because we're neighbours. You've been working hard and I thought maybe you could do with this.'

'Thank you,' she said coolly and politely, 'but there's really no need.'

He sighed. 'Nicole, I don't want to fight with you—and I could drink both espressos myself and eat both brownies, but that much caffeine and sugar in my system at once would turn me into a total nightmare. Take pity on my staff and share it with me.'

'I…'

He could see the doubt in her face, so he added, 'For Clarence and Georgy.'

She shook her head. 'Forget Georgy. She doesn't exist. Any more than Clarence does.'

'We do exist—we're real. And can you please just take the coffee and cake instead of being stubborn and stroppy? They don't come with strings attached.'

She stared at him. Just when he was about to give up and walk away, she gave the tiniest nod. 'I guess. Thank you.' She took the coffee and the brownie. 'Though actually I do feel beholden to you now.'

'There's no need. It's just coffee. As I said, no strings. I'm being neighbourly.'

'I guess I should be neighbourly, too, and invite you to sit down—' she gestured to his suit '—but you're really not dressed for this place.'

'Maybe.' He noticed that she was wearing jeans and another old T-shirt, teamed with canvas shoes; her hair was pulled back tightly into a bun. Out of habit from her banking days, or just to try and stop herself getting so dusty? Who was the real Nicole—the banker, or the girl who dreamed of the stars?

'I was just working through here.'

Gabriel followed her through into the foyer, where she'd set up a makeshift desk at one of the tables. She'd taken down the boarding on one of the windows to let some light in.

'Lighting not working?' he asked.

'The electricity supply's due to be reconnected some time today,' she said. 'I'm using a torch and this window until then.'

'And you have some spare fuses in case some of the circuits blow when the electricity's back on?'

She folded her arms and gave him a narrow-eyed look. 'I might be female, Mr Hunter, but I'm neither stupid nor helpless.'

He sighed. 'That wasn't what I was implying. You know I know you're not stupid or helpless. What I'm saying is that I have a couple of electricians next door if you run into problems, OK?'

'Since when does a hard-headed businessman offer help to the business next door?'

When it was owned by a friend, one whom he happened to know was doing this single-handedly. Not that he thought she'd accept that. And part of him thought that he was crazy. Why *would* he help her, when he wanted her to sell the place to him? He ought to be making life hard for her, not bringing her coffee and offering help from his staff.

Yet part of him wondered—was there a compromise? Could he forge a deal that would both please his father *and* help his friend? 'Damage limitation,' he said. 'If your place goes up in smoke, it's going to affect mine.' It was true. The fact that he couldn't quite separate Nicole from Georgygirl was irrelevant.

'Right.' She grabbed a cloth and rubbed the worst of the dust from one of the chairs. 'Since you're here, have a seat.'

'Thank you.' He sat down.

'So why are you really here?' she asked.

Because he missed her. But he didn't think she was ready to hear that. He wasn't sure he was ready to hear that, either. 'Being neighbourly. Just as you'd do if you were a lot further on in the restoration here and I'd just started up next door.'

'With the exception that I wouldn't be trying to buy your hotel so I could raze it to the ground to make a car park for my cinema,' she pointed out.

'I did say that was one option. There are others,' he said mildly. He just hadn't thought them all through yet. He wanted the land for car parking. Restoring the cinema instead and using it as part of the hotel was unlikely to be cost effective. To give himself some breathing space, he asked, 'Why did you call yourself Georgygirl on the forum?'

It was the last question Nicole had expected. She frowned. 'What's that got to do with the cinema?'

'Nothing. I'm just curious. Before I knew who you were, I assumed maybe your name was Georgina, or your surname was George. And then afterwards I thought of the film.'

'A film that's half a century old and has never been remade—and you loathe romcoms anyway.' Or, at least, Clarence did. She didn't know what Gabriel Hunter liked. How much of Clarence had been real?

'OK. So I looked it up on the internet. But the synopsis I read—well, it doesn't fit you. And neither does the song. You're not dowdy and any male with red blood would give you a second glance.'

'I wasn't fishing for compliments,' she said crisply. 'For the record, I'm not interested in flattery, either.'

'I was merely stating facts. Though there is one thing,' he said. 'You're Nicole on the outside and Georgy on the inside.'

Two parts of the same person. Was it the same for him? Was the nice side of Gabriel Hunter—Clarence—real? But he'd lied to her. How could she trust him? Especially as she'd made that mistake before: putting her trust in the wrong man.

She'd promised herself she'd never repeat that mistake again.

'So—why Georgygirl?' he asked again.

'It's not from that film. If you must know, it's George, as in Banks, because I'm—well, was—a banker, and girl because I'm female.'

'George Banks from *Mary Poppins*,' he said. 'I don't think you'd believe that feeding the birds is a waste—so I'm guessing that you never find the time to fly kites.'

'Clever.' And a little too close to the truth for her comfort. 'So why did you call yourself Clarence?'

'Because my name's Gabriel.'

She frowned. 'I'm not following you.'

'As in the angel,' he said.

She scoffed. 'You're no angel.'

'I don't pretend to be. I just happen to have the name of an angel.'

The Archangel Gabriel; and an angel called Clarence. '*It's a Wonderful Life*.' Her favourite film: the one she watched with her mother every Christmas Eve and wept over every time the townsfolk of Bedford Falls all came with their savings to help George Bailey. She shook her head. 'No. You should've called yourself Potter.'

'Harry?'

'Henry,' she corrected.

He grimaced. 'I know you think I'm a corporate shark, but I'd never cheat or steal like Henry Potter.' He looked her straight in the eye. 'For the record, that wasn't my teenage mistake, or have you already checked that out?'

'Once I found out who you really were, I looked you up,' she admitted. 'I saw what the papers said about you.'

'It is what it is.' He shrugged. 'So now you know the worst of me.'

'Yes. It's a hell of a teenage mistake, crashing your car into someone's shop.'

'While drunk. Don't forget that. And my father had enough money to hire a top-class lawyer who could get me off on a technicality. Which makes me the lowest of the low.' He suddenly looked really vulnerable. 'And you think I don't know that?'

She winced. Clarence had told her he regretted his teenage mistake bitterly. That he was still paying for his mistake over and over again. There was a lot more to this than the papers had reported, she was sure.

And she'd just been really, really mean to him. To the man who'd made her life that bit brighter over the last six months. How horrible did that make her?

Then again, Gabriel had tried to leverage their friendship to make her sell the cinema to him. Which made him as much of a user as Jeff. And that was something she found hard to forgive.

'Mr Hunter, we really have nothing to say to each other.'

'Georgy—Nicole,' he corrected himself, 'we've talked every night for months and I think that's real.'

'But your company wants to buy my cinema.'

'Yes.'

'It's not for sale. Not now, and not ever.'

'Message received and understood,' he said. 'Have you spoken to a surveyor yet?'

'No,' she admitted.

'I can give you some names.'

'I bet you can.'

He frowned. 'What's that supposed to mean?'

'A surveyor who'll tell me that there's so much wrong, the best thing I can do is raze it to the ground and sell you the site as a car park for your new hotel?' she asked waspishly.

'No. I'm really not like Henry Potter,' he said again. 'I was trying to be nice. To help you, because I have experience in the area and you don't.'

'Why would you help me when we're business rivals?'

'Because we don't have to be rivals,' he said. 'Maybe we can work together.'

'How?'

'What do you intend to do with the place?'

'You've already asked me that, and my answer's the same.' She looked at him. 'Would you tell a business rival what your strategy was?'

He sighed. 'Nicole, I'm not asking for rivalry reasons. I'm asking, are you going to run it as a cinema or are you going to use the space for something else? You once said if you could do anything you wanted, you'd open a café and have a space where people could do some kind of art.'

'It's a possibility,' she allowed. 'I need to sort

out my costings first and work out the best use of the space.' And she really had to make this work. She didn't want to lose all her savings and her security—to risk being as vulnerable as her mother had been when Nicole was growing up, having no choices in what she did.

'If you want to set up an art café,' he said, 'maybe I can help you find better premises for it.'

'And sell you the cinema? We've already discussed this, and you can ask me again and again until you're blue in the face, but it's not happening. Whatever I do, it'll be done right here.'

'OK. Well, as a Surrey Quays resident—'

'You mean you actually live here?' she broke in. 'You didn't just join the forum to listen out for people protesting against your development so you could charm them out of it?'

He winced. 'That was one of the reasons I joined the forum initially, I admit.'

So she'd been right and their whole relationship had been based on a lie. Just as it had with Jeff. Would she never learn?

'But I do live in Surrey Quays,' he said, and named one of the most prestigious developments on the edge of the river. 'I moved there eighteen months ago. And I'm curious about the cinema now I'm here. It's been boarded up ever since I've lived in the area.'

'You seriously expect me to give you a guided tour?'

'Would you give Clarence a tour?' he asked.

Yes. Without a shadow of a doubt. She blew out a breath. 'You're not Clarence.'

'But I am,' he said softly. 'I know things about you that you haven't told anyone else—just as you know things about me. We're friends.'

Was that true? Could she trust him?

Part of her wanted to believe that her friendship with Clarence wasn't a castle built on sand; part of her wanted to run as fast as she could in the opposite direction.

Hope had a brief tussle with common sense—and won. 'All right. I'll show you round. But it'll have to be by torchlight,' she warned.

'Cinemas are supposed to be dark,' he said with a smile.

She wished he hadn't smiled like that. It gave her goose-bumps. Gabriel Hunter had a seriously beautiful mouth, and his eyes were the colour of cornflowers.

And why was she mooning over him? Ridiculous. She needed to get a grip. Right now. 'This is the foyer—well, obviously,' she said gruffly, and shone the torch round.

He gave an audible intake of breath. 'The glass, Nicole—it's beautiful. Art Deco. It deserves to be showcased.'

The same thing she'd noticed. Warmth flared through her, and she had to damp it down. This was her business rival Gabriel Hunter, not her friend Clarence, she reminded herself.

'The cinema itself is through here.'

He sniffed as she ushered him through to the auditorium, then pulled a face. 'I'm afraid you've got a mouse problem. That's a pretty distinctive smell.'

'They've chomped the seats a lot, too.' She shone a torch onto one of the worst bits to show him.

'There are people who can restore that. I know some good upholst—' He stopped. 'Sorry. I'll shut up. You're perfectly capable of researching your own contractors.'

She brought him back out into the foyer. 'From what you said the other day, you know that this place was originally an Edwardian *kursaal* or leisure centre. The downstairs was originally a skating rink and the upstairs was the Electric Cinema.'

'Does that mean you have a projection room upstairs as well as down?' he asked.

'I'm still mapping the place out and working my way through all the junk, but I think so—because in the nineteen-thirties it was changed to a ballroom upstairs and a picture house downstairs.'

'So is upstairs still the ballroom?'

Upstairs was the bit that she hoped would make him change his mind about ever asking her to sell again. Because surely, working for a company which renovated old buildings and redeveloped them into hotels, he must have some appreciation of architecture? Clarence would love it, she knew; but how much of Clarence had been designed simply to charm her and how much of Clarence was really Gabriel? That was what she hadn't worked out yet. And until she did she wasn't prepared to give him the benefit of the doubt.

'The stairs,' she said, gesturing towards them.

'That's beautiful, too. Look at that railing. I can imagine women sweeping down that staircase in floaty dresses after waltzing the night away.'

Just as she'd thought when she'd seen the staircase. And there was no way that Gabriel could've known she'd thought that, because she hadn't told him. So was his response pure Clarence, and that meant Clarence was the real part of him, after all?

'And this room at the top,' she said as they walked up the stairs, 'was used by Brian as a store-room, or so Mum says.'

'Is your mum OK?' he asked.

She frowned. 'OK about what?'

'This place. It must have memories for her. And, in the circumstances…' His voice faded.

'She's fine. But thank you for asking.'

'I wasn't being polite, and I wasn't asking for leverage purposes, either,' he said softly. 'I was asking as your friend, Nicole.'

Gabriel wasn't her friend, though.

Saying nothing, she opened the door to the upper room and handed him the torch. 'See what you think.'

He shone the torch on the flooring first. 'That looks like parquet flooring—cleaned up, that will be stunning.' He bent down to take a closer look. 'Just look at the inlay—Nicole, this is gorgeous.'

But it wasn't the really stunning bit of the room. She still couldn't understand why her grandfather had wasted it by using the room as storage space.

'Look up,' she said.

Gabriel shone the torch upwards and she actually heard his intake of breath. 'Is that plasterwork or is it pressed tin?' he asked.

'I assume it's plasterwork. I didn't even know ceilings could be made of anything else. Well, except maybe wood?'

'Do you have a ladder?' he asked.

'It doesn't tend to be something that a banker would use in their everyday job, so no,' she said dryly.

'I'll bring one over from next door later this afternoon, so we can take a closer look,' he said.

We? she wondered. It was *her* cinema, not his. But at least he seemed to appreciate the ceiling.

'Do you still want to raze the place to the ground, then?' she asked.

'No,' he admitted. 'If that ceiling's tin, which I think it might be, that's quite rare in England and it'll probably get this building listed. Look at those Art Deco stars—they're absolutely amazing.'

He'd already told her that if a building was listed it meant extra work and delays. 'You mean, that ceiling will get the building listed if someone drops the council an anonymous letter telling them about it?' she asked sharply.

'If you mean me or anyone at Hunter's, no. That's not how I operate. But I've got experience in this sort of thing, Nicole. I can help you. We're not on opposite sides.'

'It feels like it.'

'We've been friends for a while. We probably know more about each other than most of our non-online friends know about us.'

'But do we really?' she asked. 'How do we know it wasn't all an act?'

'It wasn't on my part,' he said, 'and I'm pretty sure it wasn't on yours.' He held her gaze. 'Have dinner with me tonight.'

No. Common sense meant that she should say no.

But the expression in his eyes wasn't one of triumph or guile. She couldn't quite read it.

'Why do you want to have dinner with me?' she asked.

Gabriel couldn't blame her for being suspicious. He *had* been trying to buy her cinema, planning to turn it into a car park for his hotel. But now he'd seen the building and its potential he was looking at the whole thing in a different light. Maybe there was a way to compromise. OK, so he wouldn't get the parking, but he might get something even better. Something that would benefit them both.

'Because then we can talk. Properly.' He sighed. 'Look, you know my background's in the service and entertainment industry. I've worked with several renovations, bringing a building kicking and screaming back to life and then into the modern age. I've got a lot of knowledge that could help you, and a lot of contacts that would be useful for you.'

'And what's in it for you?'

She was so prickly with him now. And he wanted their old easy-going relationship back. 'Does something have to be in it for me?'

'You have a reputation as a very hard-headed businessman. I can accept that you'd maybe do charity work, because that would double up as good PR for Hunter Hotels, but I'm not a charity.' She looked at him again. 'So why would you help me for nothing?'

'Because,' he said softly, 'I live in Surrey Quays and this building is part of my community. Plus Georgygirl's my friend and I'd like to help her make her dreams come true.'

'And there's really nothing in it for you? At all?'

Maybe this was the time for honesty. And she was right in that there was some self-interest. 'Do you remember suggesting to me that I ought to take the family business in a different direction—that I should do something that really interests me, something that gives me a challenge?'

'Yes.'

'Maybe this would be my challenge.'

'And that's it? To help someone you think is your friend and to give yourself an intellectual challenge?'

And to give him some freedom. But he wasn't quite ready to admit how stifled he felt. Not to Nicole. Georgy was a different matter; but right now Nicole wasn't Georgy and she didn't trust him. 'That's it,' he said. 'Have dinner with me tonight and we can discuss it properly.'

Nicole intended to say no, but the words that came out of her mouth were different. 'Only on condition we go halves on the bill tonight—and I owe you for the coffee and brownie.'

'You can buy me coffee later in the week,' he said. 'I'll be around next door.'

'You're trying to tell me you're the boy next door, now?'

He shrugged. 'My business is next to yours and I have a Y chromosome, so I guess that's the same thing.'

She shook her head. 'It's a million miles away, Mr Hunter, and you know it.'

He didn't argue with her; instead, he said, 'I'll book somewhere for dinner. I already know we both like Italian food. I'll pick you up at, what, seven?'

'I suppose you've already looked up my address,' she said, feeling slightly nettled.

'On the electoral roll, yes.' He paused. 'It would be useful to have each other's phone number in case one of us is delayed.'

'True.' And in the meantime she might be able to think up a good excuse not to meet him, and could text him said good excuse. She grabbed her phone from her pocket. 'Tell me your number, then I'll text you so you'll have mine.'

It only took a matter of seconds to sort that out.

'Thank you for showing me round,' he said. 'I'll see you later.'

'OK.'

But she couldn't stop thinking about him all afternoon. Was she doing the right thing, going to dinner with him? Could they work together?

Or was she just setting herself up for yet another fall and it'd be better to call it off?

Halfway through the afternoon there was a knock on the front door, and she heard Gabriel call, 'Hello? Nicole, are you here?'

She was about to ask what he thought he was doing when she realised that he'd changed into jeans and an old T-shirt—making him look much more approachable than his shark-in-a-suit persona—and he was carrying a ladder.

'Why the ladder?' she asked.

'Remember I said I'd bring one over? I thought we could take a closer look at your ceiling,' he said.

'Don't you need to be somewhere?'

He smiled. 'I don't have to account for every minute of my time. Anyway, I promised you a ladder. Given that you've already said a ladder isn't part of your everyday equipment—whereas it *is* part of mine—I'll carry the ladder and you do the torch?'

'No need for a torch. The electricity's back on now.'

'The fuses are OK?'

'So far, yes, but obviously I'll need to get the wiring checked out properly.'

This time he didn't offer help from his team next door; part of her was relieved that he'd got the message, but part of her was disappointed that he'd given up on her so quickly. Which was ridiculous and contrary. She didn't want to be beholden to Gabriel Hunter for anything. But she missed her friend Clarence.

'Let's go take a look at that ceiling,' he said instead.

In the old ballroom, he rested the ladder against the wall.

'So you're going to hold the ladder steady for me?' she asked.

'Do you know what to look for?' he checked.

'No, but it's my ceiling.' And she wanted to be the first one to look at it.

He grinned, as if guessing exactly what was going through her mind. 'Yes, ma'am. OK. You go up first and take a look.' He took the camera from round his neck and handed it to her. 'And photographs, if you want.'

She recognised the make of the camera as seriously expensive. 'You're trusting me with this?'

'Yes. Why wouldn't I?'

He clearly wasn't as suspicious and mean-minded as she was, which made her feel a twinge of guilt. 'Thanks,' she said. She put the camera strap round her neck so it'd leave her hands free, then climbed up the ladder. Close up, she still didn't have a clue whether she was looking at plasterwork or tin. But she duly took photographs and went back down the ladder.

Gabriel reviewed her photographs on the rear screen of the camera.

'So can you tell whether it's tin or plasterwork from the photographs?' she asked.

He shook his head. 'Would you mind if I went up and had a look?'

'Go ahead. I'll hold the ladder steady.'

As he climbed the ladder, Nicole noticed how nice his backside looked encased in faded denim. And how inappropriate was that? She damped down the unexpected flickers of desire and concentrated on holding the ladder steady.

'It's definitely pressed tin,' Gabriel said when

he came back down. 'It was very popular in early twentieth-century America because it was an affordable alternative to plasterwork, plus it was lightweight and fireproof. So I guess that's why it was used here, to keep the ceiling fireproof. The tin sheets were pressed with a die to make patterned panels, then painted white to make them look as if it was plasterwork. Though, if that's still the original paint up there, it's likely to be lead, so you need to be careful and get a specialist in to restore the panels.'

'It sounds as if you've come across this before.'

He nodded. 'There was a tin ceiling and tin wainscoting in a hotel we renovated three or four years ago. Basically you need to strip off the old paint to get rid of the lead—for health and safety reasons—then put on a protective base coat, patch up any damage and repaint it.' He paused. 'Usually the panels were painted white, but there seem to be some traces of gold on the stars.'

She looked up at the ceiling. 'I can imagine this painted dark blue, with gold stars.'

'Especially with that floor, this would really work as a ballroom—and ballroom dancing is definitely on trend. There are even fitness classes based on ballroom dance moves. You could take the *kursaal* back to its roots but bring it into this century at the same time.'

He was talking a lot of sense. Putting things into words that she'd already started to think about. 'It's a possibility.' She continued staring at the ceiling. 'There are all kinds of styles around the cinema, everything from Edwardian through to slightly shabby nineteen-seventies. It's a mess, and it'd be sensible to take it back to one point in time. And, with features like this, it'd make sense to restore the building back to how it was when it was a ballroom and cinema. It's a shame there won't be any colour pictures to give me any idea what the original decorative schemes looked like, though. There definitely isn't any paperwork giving any details.'

'Actually, there might be colour photos,' he said, and grabbed his phone. After a few seconds' browsing, he handed the phone to her so she could see for herself. 'Just as I thought. According to this website, colour photos exist from as far back as the middle of the eighteen hundreds.'

'But weren't they coloured by hand, back then—so they were colourised rather than actually being printed in colour?' Nicole pointed out.

'Look, you can see the three different print overlay colours at the edge of this one.' He pored over the screen with her. 'But it also says the process was time-consuming.'

'And expensive, so it'd be reserved for really big news stories—unless I guess someone was really wealthy and did it as a hobby. Though would they have taken a picture of the building?'

'There might be something in the local archive office,' he said. 'Photos or sketches that people haven't seen for a century.'

They looked at each other, and Nicole thought, he's as excited by this as I am. But was this Clarence standing next to her or Gabriel? She couldn't be sure. And, until she was sure, she didn't dare trust him. 'Maybe,' she said carefully.

He'd clearly picked up her wariness, because he said, 'It is as it is. I'd better let you get on. See you at seven.'

'OK.'

Though when Nicole got home it occurred to her that he hadn't told her where they were going, and she didn't have a clue whether she was supposed to dress up or dress down.

She thought about it in the shower while she was washing her hair. If she wore jeans, she'd feel uncomfortable in a posh restaurant—and would he take her somewhere posh to try to impress her? But if she dressed up, she'd feel totally out of place in a more casual bistro.

Little black dress, she decided. Something she would feel comfortable in no matter the situation. And high heels, so he'd know she wasn't intimidated by him.

Bring it on, she thought.

Bring it on.

CHAPTER FIVE

GABRIEL PARKED OUTSIDE Nicole's flat. Nerves fluttered in his stomach, which was absolutely ridiculous, and completely out of character. This wasn't a real date; it was discussing mutual business interests. There was no reason why he should be feeling like this.

Yet this was Nicole. Georgygirl.

And that made things that little bit more complicated.

He and Nicole were on opposite sides. Rivals. And yet Georgy was his friend. The girl he'd got to know over the last six months and really liked. The one person who saw him for who he really was.

How ironic that, now they'd met in real life, she didn't see him at all. She saw Gabriel Hunter, the ruthless businessman: not Clarence, her friend.

He shook himself. It was pointless brooding. Things were as they were. All he could do was make the best out of it and try to salvage a few things from this mess. Maybe he could reach a better understanding with her, in business if nothing else.

Nicole lived in a quieter part of Surrey Quays, in what he recognised as a former industrial complex that had been turned into four-storey apartment blocks. The brickwork was a mellow sand colour; one side had floor-to-ceiling windows and the three upper storeys had a wrought iron balcony. There were trees and raised planted beds in the square, and the whole thing was pretty and peaceful—exactly the kind of place where he'd expected Georgy to live.

He pressed the button to her intercom.

'I'm on my way,' she said.

Economical with words, as usual, he thought with a smile.

But he was blown away when she walked out of the doors to the apartment block. She was wearing a simple black shift dress, with high-heeled black court shoes and no jewellery. Her hair was still pulled back from her face, but this time it was in a sophisticated updo that reminded him of Audrey Hepburn.

'You look amazing,' he said, before he could stop himself.

She inclined her head. 'Thank you.'

And now he felt like he was on his first date all over again. Which was stupid, because as a teenager he'd been overconfident and reckless, never worrying about what people thought of him. He took a deep breath. 'It's only a short drive from here.'

'Short enough to make it more sensible to walk? I can change my shoes.'

'We'll drive,' he said.

He half expected her to make an acerbic comment about his car—a sleek convertible—but she climbed into the passenger seat and said nothing. It wasn't exactly an easy silence between them, but he had no idea what to say, so he concentrated on driving. And she did nothing to dispel the awkwardness between them, either.

Was this a mistake?

Or was she as confused by this whole thing as he was?

Once he'd parked and they were out of the car, he gestured to the narrowboat moored at the quay. 'The food at this place is excellent,' he said.

She read the sign out loud. 'La Chiatta.'

'Italian for "the barge",' he translated.

'Effective.' But then she looked at the narrowboat and the ramp which led from the quay to the deck. The tide was low, so the angle of the ramp was particularly steep. From the expression on her face, Nicole clearly realised she wouldn't be able to walk down that ramp in high heels. Although clothing was something they'd never really talked about in their late-night conversations, Gabriel had the strongest feeling that Nicole almost never wore high heels and had only worn them tonight to prove a point.

'We have two choices,' he said. 'We can go somewhere else that doesn't have a ramp.'

'But you've booked here, yes? It's not fair to the restaurant if we just don't turn up.'

He shrugged. 'I'll pay them a cancellation fee so they don't lose out.'

'What's the second choice?'

Something that would probably get him into trouble, but he couldn't stop himself. 'This,' he said, and picked her up.

'Gabriel!'

It was the first time she'd used his given name and he rather liked it.

But maybe picking her up had been a mistake. Not because she was too heavy, but because she was so close that he could feel the warmth of her skin and smell the soft floral scent of her perfume, and it made him want to kiss her.

That was so inappropriate, it was untrue.

'Hold on tight,' he said, and carried her down the ramp before setting her on her feet again.

'I don't believe you just did that,' she said, sounding shocked.

Clearly tonight she was seeing him as Gabriel the corporate shark, not Clarence. 'No, it was a solution to a problem. By the time we've finished dinner the tide will have changed and you'll be able to walk up the ramp relatively easily.'

She gestured towards the ramp, where a man

and a woman were gingerly making their way down together. 'He's not carrying her.'

'Probably because she's wearing flat shoes. No way could you have walked down that ramp in *those* without falling over.' He gestured to her shoes.

'You could've warned me.'

'I didn't even think about it,' he admitted.

'Or I could have taken off my shoes just now.'

'And ended up standing on a sharp stone or something and hurting yourself? My way was simpler, and it's done now so there's no point in arguing about it.'

'If you say, "It is what it is",' she warned, 'I might just punch you.'

He laughed. 'Think about it. It's true. Come and have dinner, Nicole. Have you been here before?'

'No.'

'The pasta is amazing.'

She didn't looked particularly mollified, but she thanked him politely for opening the door for her and walked inside.

* * *

This was supposed to be a business discussion, Nicole thought, so why did it feel like a date?

And she still couldn't quite get over what Gabriel had just done on the ramp. Even Jeff, back in the days when she was still in ignorant bliss of his affair and trusted him, wouldn't have done something like that.

What was worse was that she'd liked being close to Gabriel—close enough to feel the warmth of his skin and smell the citrusy scent of whatever shower gel he used.

And, just before he'd set her back down on her feet, she'd actually wondered what it would be like if he kissed her.

She needed to get this out of her head right now. They weren't friends and they weren't dating; this was strictly business.

Once the waitress had brought their menus and she'd ordered a glass of red wine—noting that Gabriel was sticking to soft drinks—she looked at him. 'Is there anything in particular you recommend?'

'The honeycomb cannelloni is pretty good, and their ciabatta bread is amazing.'

'Sounds good.' At least their tastes meshed when it came to food. He hadn't lied to her about that, then.

Once the waitress had taken their order, he leaned back in his chair. 'Thank you for agreeing to meet me tonight, Nicole.'

'As you say, it's business and neither of us has time to waste. We might as well eat while we discuss things, and save a bit of time.'

She really hoped that it didn't show in her voice how much she was having to fight that spark of attraction. She was absolutely *not* going to let herself wonder what it would be like to run her fingers through his hair, or how the muscles of his back would feel beneath her fingertips.

To distract herself, she asked, 'So what really happened?'

He looked puzzled. 'When?'

'Your teenage incident.'

Gabriel really hadn't expected her to bring that up. Where was she going with this? Was it to distract him and make him agree to a business deal that, in a saner moment, he would never even have considered? Or maybe he was just being cynical because he'd spent too long in a ruthless business world. Maybe she really did want to know. He shrugged. 'You said you'd read up about it, so you already know the details.'

'I know what was reported, which isn't necessarily the same thing.'

That surprised him, too. She was more perceptive than he'd expected. Then again, how could he tell her the truth? It felt like bleating. And at the end of the day he was the one who'd done something wrong. He shrugged again. 'I was nineteen years old, from a wealthy and privileged background and full of testosterone. My whole crowd was identikit. I guess we all thought we were invincible.'

'I don't buy it,' she said.

'Why not?'

'It was your car, right?'

'Yes,' he admitted.

'Even full of testosterone, I don't think you would've been stupid enough to get behind the steering wheel of a car if you'd been drinking.' She gestured to his glass of mineral water. 'And I notice you're not even having one glass of wine now—which I assume is because you're driving.'

It warmed him. Even if Nicole did see him as her business rival, someone she shouldn't even like, she was being fair to him. And she'd picked up on the thing that the newspapers hadn't. 'It is. I wouldn't put anyone at risk like that.'

'So what really happened?'

He shook his head. 'It doesn't matter now. I was the one behind the wheel with alcohol in my bloodstream, I was the one who crashed into the shop, and I was the one whose father's expensive lawyer got me off on a technicality. It was my fault.'

'You didn't actually know you'd been drinking, did you?'

He knew she was perceptive, but that really shocked him. 'What makes you say that?' he asked carefully.

'Because,' she said, 'even given that you might've had a lot of growing up to do back then, there's a massive difference between high spirits and stupidity, and you're not stupid. Not with the highest First your university had ever awarded and an MBA from the best business school in the country.'

'So you really did do some digging on me.' He wasn't sure if he was more impressed or discomfited.

'Just as you did on me,' she pointed out, 'so get off your high horse and answer the question.'

'You're right. I didn't know I'd been drinking,' he said. 'I assume there was vodka in my orange juice—something I wouldn't have tasted.'

'So the people who spiked your drink got away with it.'

'I got away with it, too,' he reminded her. 'On a technicality.'

'Maybe Gabriel did,' she said. 'But I know a different side to you.'

She was actually recognising who he was? Gabriel was stunned into silence.

'You've stuck out a job you don't enjoy, out of loyalty,' she continued, 'because your dad sorted out the mess you made, so you didn't have a criminal record and could finish your law degree. And

I think Clarence would've done something more. At the very least, Clarence would've gone to see the shop owners and apologised.'

He squirmed. Now he really understood why she'd made it up the ranks so swiftly at the bank, despite not having a degree. She was the most clear-sighted person he'd ever met. 'Do we have to talk about this?' Because he could see where this was going, and it made him antsy.

'If we're really going to work together in any way, shape or form,' she said, 'I need to know who you are. Are you the heir to Hunter Hotels, who dates a different woman every week?'

'Strictly speaking, I haven't dated at all for the last six months.' Since he'd first started talking to her online. Which hadn't actually occurred to him until now. Was that why he hadn't dated? Because part of him was already involved with her?

'Or are you really my friend Clarence?' she asked.

'It's not that black and white,' he said. Part of him was Gabriel, the heir to Hunter Hotels, desperate to make up for his past mistakes and yet feeling stifled. And part of him was Clarence, a man who actually connected with people around him. If the crash hadn't happened, what would his life have been like? He wouldn't have had to spend so much time biting his tongue and reminding himself to be grateful. Maybe he could've been Clarence all the time. 'I could ask you the same. Are you Nicole Thomas, the workaholic banker, or are you Georgygirl, who dreams of the stars?' He paused. 'And you've got the stars, right on the ceiling of your cinema.'

'Maybe I'm a bit of both,' she said.

'And so,' he said, 'am I.'

'So what did you do?'

He sighed. 'You're not going to let this go, are you? Nicole, it's not public knowledge and I want it to stay that way.'

'Who else knows?'

'Two others.'

'Not your father?'

'No,' he admitted. Evan Hunter had decreed that everything was done and dusted. The shopkeeper had been paid off, Gabriel didn't have a criminal record and, although Evan hadn't said it in so many words, Gabriel would be paying for that mistake for the rest of his life. He certainly had, to date. And he felt as if he'd never earn his father's respect.

'The shopkeeper, then,' Nicole said. 'And his wife.'

She was good, he thought. Incisive. Good at reading people and situations. 'I'm saying nothing until I know this stays with you,' he said.

'Do you trust me?'

'Do you trust me?' he countered.

She sighed. 'We're back to the online-or-real-life thing. Two different people.'

'Are we? Because I'd trust Georgygirl and I think you'd trust Clarence.'

She spread her hands. 'OK. It's your decision.'

If he told her, it would give her leverage.

If he didn't, it would tell her that he didn't trust her and she couldn't trust him.

He thought about it. Was it a risk worth taking? Strategically, it meant giving a little now to gain a lot in the future.

'Obviously my father paid for the damage to the shop,' he said. 'But you can't solve everything with money.'

'So what did you do?' Her voice was very soft. Gentle. Not judgemental. And that made it easier to tell her.

'I went to see the Khans,' he said. 'With a big bouquet of flowers and a genuine apology. And I said that money alone wasn't enough to repay the damage I'd done, so until the end of my degree I'd work weekends in their shop, unpaid, doing whatever needed doing.'

'Stocking shelves?'

'Sometimes. And sorting out the newspapers for the delivery boys—which meant getting there at five in the morning. And don't forget sweeping the floor and cleaning out the fridges.'

She raised her eyebrows. 'It must've killed your partying, having to be at work for five in the morning at weekends.'

'The crash kind of did that anyway,' he said. 'It was my wake-up call.'

She looked straight at him. 'You weren't just a shop-boy, were you?'

'I was at first,' he said. 'It was six months before the Khans started to believe that I wasn't just a posh boy slumming it, but eventually I became their friend.' He smiled. 'I used to eat with them on Sundays after my shift in the shop. Meera taught me how to make a seriously good biryani, and Vijay taught me as much as my father did about business management and having to understand your own business right from the bottom up. Though in return when I did my MBA I helped them streamline a few processes and negotiate better terms with their suppliers.'

'Do you still see them?'

'Not as often nowadays, but yes. Their kids are teenagers now; they were very small when the crash happened. Sanjay, their eldest, is off to university next year, and I've given him the lecture about partying and getting in with the wrong crowd.' As well as sponsoring the boy through the three years of his degree, but Nicole didn't need to know that.

When the food arrived, she tasted her cannelloni and looked thoughtful.

'Is it OK?' he asked.

'More than OK. You were right about the food, just as you were right about the coffee on Challoner Road.' She paused. 'What you did for the Khans…that's what I'd expect Clarence to do.'

'Clarence wouldn't have been stupid enough to go round with the over-privileged crowd in the first place,' he pointed out.

'You're human. We all make mistakes.'

Which revealed that she had a weakness, too. That she'd made a life-changing mistake. One that maybe held her back as much as his did him.

'What was yours?' he asked softly.

She shook her head. 'It's not important.'

'I told you mine. Fair's fair.'

She looked away. 'Let's just say I put my trust in the wrong person.'

'And you think I'm going to let you down, the same way?'

She spread her hands. 'Gabriel Hunter, known for being a ruthless businessman—is it any wonder I think his offer of help with the cinema comes with strings?'

'Or you could see it as Clarence,' he countered, 'who really needs a new challenge, and a way to take the family business in a different direction.'

'OK. Just supposing the Electric Palace was yours…what would you do?'

'Bring the building back to life, and then get it listed so nobody can ever try to raze it to the ground and turn it into a car park,' he said promptly. 'In that order.'

She smiled. 'Right. But seriously?'

'You've got two main rooms, both with projectors, yes?'

'Yes?'

'Do you know the capacity of the rooms?'

'There are three hundred and fifty seats in the lower room.'

'The upper room's smaller. We'd need to measure it properly, but I'd guess we could fit seventy-five to a hundred.' He looked thoughtful. 'I really like your idea of taking the Electric Palace back to how it was when it was first built. You've got the ceiling upstairs, the parquet flooring and the amazing glass in the foyer. We need to look in the archives and ask on the Surrey Quays forum to see if anyone's got any old newspapers or magazines, or anything that has pictures or sketches or a detailed description of how it was.'

'But originally it was a cinema and ice rink,' she reminded him.

'I don't think an ice rink would bring in enough footfall or spend,' he said. 'The next incarnation would work better—the cinema and the ballroom. But keep the Art Deco glass. That's too stunning to lose.'

'You really want to turn the upstairs room back into the ballroom?'

'No. I think it'd work better as a multi-purpose room,' he said. 'If you didn't have fixed seats, you could use it as a cinema; but you could also use it as a ballroom and a conference venue.'

'Conference venue?' she asked.

He knew he was probably speaking too soon, but it was the perfect solution. A way to work together, so he could help his friend *and* impress his father. 'Conference venue,' he confirmed. 'The chairs you use for the cinema—they could be placed around the edge of the dance floor on ballroom nights, and they could be moved easily into whatever configuration you need for a conference, whether it was horseshoe or theatre-style. And if you use tables that fit together, they'd also work as occasional tables for the cinema and ballroom nights.' He warmed to his theme. 'Or for any club that wants to hire the room—you could still do the craft stuff. Offer people crafternoon tea.'

'Crafternoon tea?' She looked mystified.

'A session of craft—whether it's sewing or painting or pottery—followed by afternoon tea. Hence crafternoon tea,' he explained.

'That's the most terrible pun I've ever heard,' she said. 'Maybe. But would anyone really hire that room for a conference? I can't see it.'

'You have a hotel next door,' he said. 'Which would hire the room as a main conference suite, and there could be breakout rooms for the conference next door.'

'What about refreshments and meals for the conference delegates?'

'Depends on your staff and facilities. That's when we'd work together,' he said. 'We'd have to sort out costings and come up with something that was fair to both of us. I'm thinking out loud, here, but maybe you'd do the coffee and a buffet lunch, and I'd do the evening sit-down meal, because my kitchen has a bigger capacity than yours.'

'Right,' she said.

'And then there's downstairs,' he said, ignoring the fact that she didn't seem enthusiastic—once he'd worked out the costings and she could see it would benefit both of them, she'd come round. 'We have the main cinema. We can restore the seats. As I said, I know specialist upholsterers who can do that.'

'The seats are old and uncomfortable. The multiplexes offer VIP seating. Maybe that's the sort of thing I should put in.'

He shook his head. 'We can't compete with the multiplexes, not with one full-time and one part-time screen. They have twenty or more screens and can offer staggered film times. We can't.'

'So maybe we need to offer something different.'

He wondered if she realised that she was using the word 'we'. Though he wasn't going to call her on it, and risk her backing away again. 'Such as?'

'When I was looking at what my competitors offer, I saw an idea I really liked—a place that had comfortable sofas instead of traditional cinema seating, and little tables where people could put their drinks or food,' she said.

'Like having the best night in, except you've gone out for it?' he asked. 'So you've got all the comfort and convenience of home, but professional quality sound and vision—actually, that would work really well.'

'And when the ushers take you to your seat, they also offer to take your order for food and drink. Which they bring to you and put on the little table.'

'I like that. A lot. But serving alcohol and hot food means getting a licence,' he said, 'and we'd have to think about what we offer on the menu.'

'We could have cinema-themed food,' she said. 'But it has to be easy to eat. Pizza, burgers, hot dogs and chicken.'

'Would that replace traditional cinema snacks?'

'No. Not everyone would want a meal. I think we need to include the traditional stuff, too—popcorn, nachos, bags of chocolates. And tubs of ice cream from a local supplier.'

Her eyes were shining. He'd just bet his were

the same. Brainstorming ideas with her was the most enjoyment he'd had from anything work-related in a long, long time. And he had a feeling it was the same for her.

'You know what this is like?' he asked.

'What?'

'Talking to you online. But better, because it's face to face.'

Then he wished he hadn't said anything when she looked wary again.

'Excuse me,' she said. 'I need the Ladies'.'

'The toilets are that way.' He indicated in the direction behind her.

'Thanks.'

On her way to the toilets, Nicole stopped by the till and handed over her credit card. 'Mr Hunter's table,' she said. 'The bill's mine. Please make sure that you charge everything to me.'

'Of course, madam,' the waiter said.

She smiled. 'Thanks.' It would save any argument over the bill later. And, given that Gabriel had already bought her two coffees and a brownie, she felt in his debt. This would even things out a little.

You know what this is like? Talking to you online. But better. His words echoed in her head.

He was right.

And she really didn't know what to do about it, which was why she'd been a coward and escaped to the toilets.

Tonight, Gabriel wasn't the corporate shark-in-a-suit; he was wearing a casual shirt and chinos that made him far more approachable. He'd attracted admiring glances from every single female in the restaurant—and it wasn't surprising. Gabriel Hunter was absolutely gorgeous.

But.

They were still on opposite sides. They shouldn't be wanting to have anything to do with each other, let alone help each other. And could she trust him? Or would he let her down as badly as Jeff had?

She still didn't have an answer by the time she returned to their table. And she was quiet all through pudding.

And when he discovered that she'd already paid

the bill, he looked seriously fed up. 'Dinner was my idea, Nicole. I was going to pay.'

'And I told you, the deal was that we went halves.'

'So why did you pay for the whole lot?'

'Because you bought me two coffees and a brownie, and I don't like being in anyone's debt. I pay my way.'

'Now I'm in your debt.'

She smiled. 'That suits me.'

'It doesn't suit me. And we haven't really finished our conversation.'

Excitement fluttered in her stomach. So what was he going to suggest now? Another business meeting over dinner? Coffee at his place?

'We kind of have,' she said. 'You've agreed that the Electric Palace should be restored, and you know it's not for sale.'

'But,' he said, 'we haven't agreed terms for conference hire, or whether you're going to use my kitchen facilities to save having to build your own.'

'That assumes I'm going to develop the cinema the way you see it. I have my own ideas.' At the end of the day, this was *her* business. She'd spent ten years marching to someone else's tune, and she wasn't about to let Gabriel take over—even if he did have more experience than she did.

'I think we need another meeting,' he said.

He looked all cool and calm and controlled. And Nicole really wanted to see him ruffled.

But maybe that was the red wine talking. Even though she'd stuck to her limit of no more than one glass. Cool, calm and controlled would be better for both of them.

'I don't have my diary on me,' she said.

His expression very clearly said he didn't believe a word of it, but he spread his hands. 'Text me some times and dates.'

So now the ball was in her court?

She could turn him down.

Or they could explore this. See where the business was going.

See where they were going.

She damped down the little flicker of hope. She couldn't trust him that far. Jeff had destroyed her ability to trust.

'I'll text you,' she said. Because that gave her

wriggle room. A chance to say no when she'd had time to think about it on her own. Gabriel was charming and persuasive; Jeff had been charming and persuasive, too, and following his ideas had got her badly burned. Who was to say that this wouldn't be the same?

'Good.'

The ramp was much more manageable now the tide had turned, and this time Gabriel didn't sweep her off her feet. Nicole wasn't sure whether she was more relieved or disappointed. And he didn't suggest coffee at his place; she wasn't quite ready to offer him coffee at hers. So he merely saw her to the door of her apartment block—brushing off her protests that she was perfectly capable of seeing herself home from the car park with a blunt, 'It's basic good manners.'

And he didn't try to kiss her goodnight, not even with a peck on the cheek.

Which was a good thing, she told herself. They didn't have that kind of relationship. Besides, she wasn't good at relationships. Hadn't Jeff's mistress said that Nicole was a cold fish? So looking for anything else from this would be a huge mistake. It would be better to keep things strictly business. And, even better than that, to keep her distance from him completely.

CHAPTER SIX

'HELLO? IS ANYONE THERE?'

Nicole went in search of the voice, to discover a man standing in the entrance to the cinema, holding a metal box of tools.

'Are you Nicole Thomas?' he asked.

'Yes,' she said.

'I'm Kyle. The boss wants me to do a quick check on your wiring.'

'Boss?' Did he mean Gabriel? But she hadn't asked Gabriel for help—and this felt a bit as if he was trying to take over.

She thought quickly to find a polite way to refuse, and it clearly showed on her face because Kyle said, 'The boss said you'd tell me thank you but you don't need any help, and he says to tell you he wants me to check your wiring's OK to make sure this place doesn't burn down and set his hotel on fire.'

It was a comment that Gabriel had made before. It wasn't something she could counter easily, and this would either reassure her or be an early warning of difficulties to come. Plus it wasn't Kyle's fault that Gabriel made her antsy. She smiled at him. 'OK. Thank you. Can I offer you a coffee? I'm sorry, I don't have any milk or sugar.'

'You're all right. I just had my tea break next door.'

'Right. Um, I guess I need to show you where the fuse box is, to start with?'

'That, and I'll check a few of the sockets to be on the safe side.'

She showed him where the fuse box was, and left him to get on with it.

He came to find her when he'd finished. 'There's good news and bad,' he said.

'Tell me the bad, first,' she said.

'You've got a bit of mouse damage to some of the cabling around the fuse box, because it was an area they could get to.'

'Will it take long to fix?'

He shook his head. 'And the good news is the wiring's been redone at some point in the last thirty years. You haven't got any aluminium cable, lead-sheathed cable or the old black cables with a rubber sheath which would mean it was really old and could burn the place down. I would recommend getting a full system check, though, when you get that little bit of cabling replaced.'

'Thank you. That's good to know. I appreciate your help.'

'No worries.' He sketched a salute and left.

Nicole made a mental note to call in to the hotel later that afternoon with a tin of chocolate biscuits to say thanks. Though she knew who she really needed to thank. Strictly speaking, it was interference, but she knew Gabriel had only done it to help—and he'd dressed it in a way that meant she could accept it. She grabbed her phone and called him. 'Thank you for sending over your electrician.'

'Pleasure. So you didn't send him away with a flea in his ear?' Gabriel asked.

'You kind of pre-empted me on that.'

'Ah, the "I don't want you to set my hotel on fire" thing. And it's true. Total self-interest on my part.' He laughed. 'So how is the wiring?'

'Apparently there's a bit of mouse damage so I'll need to replace some of the cabling, but the good news is that it's modern cable so I'm not looking at a total rewire.'

'That's great. Have you sorted out a surveyor yet?'

'I have three names.' Though she knew she was working quite a way out of her experience zone. Although she wanted to keep her independence and sort out everything herself, was that really the right thing for her business? It would be sensible to ask for advice from someone who knew that area—like Gabriel—instead of being too proud and then making a mistake that could jeopardise the cinema. Asking for help would be pragmatic, not weak. Suggesting they got together to talk about it wasn't the same as suggesting a date. And it wasn't just an excuse to see him. It really wasn't, she told herself firmly. She wasn't going to let her attraction to him derail the cinema restoration project. She cleared her throat. 'I was wondering if maybe I could buy you a coffee and run the names by you.'

'Strictly speaking, I'm the one beholden to you and ought to be the one buying the coffee. You paid for dinner last night,' he reminded her.

'You paid for coffee twice. I still owe you coffee twice.'

'In which case I owe you dinner. When are you free?'

Help. That felt much more like a date. And she wasn't ready. 'Let's focus on the coffee,' she said. 'When are you at the hotel next?'

'About half-past two this afternoon.'

'The perfect time for a coffee break. See you then.'

And it was as easy as that. She knew how he liked his coffee. She also knew he had a weakness for chocolate brownies, as long as it was dark chocolate. So, at twenty-nine minutes past two, Nicole walked in to the building site next door with two espressos, two brownies and a tin of chocolate biscuits, and asked the first person she saw to point her in the direction of Gabriel Hunter.

He was in a room which was clearly earmarked as a future office, and he was on the phone when she arrived; he lifted his hand in acknowledgement, and she waited in the corridor until he'd finished the call, to give him some privacy.

'Good to see you, Nicole,' he said.

Was that Clarence talking, or Gabriel the shark-in-a-suit? 'Coffee and a brownie,' she said, handing them over. 'And these biscuits are for Kyle, your electrician. To say thank you for checking out my wiring.'

'I'll make sure he gets them. And thank you for the coffee. Having a good day?' he asked, smiling at her.

That definitely sounded more like Clarence speaking. And the way he smiled made her stomach flip. With a real effort, Nicole forced herself to focus on business. 'Yes. How about you?'

He shrugged. 'It is as it is.'

His eyes really were beautiful. So was his mouth. It would be so very, very easy to reach out and trace his lower lip with her fingertip…

And it would also be insane. To distract herself, Nicole muttered, 'As I said, I've got to the stage where I need a surveyor and quotes from builders.'

'Obviously you know to add at least ten per cent to any quote, because with a renovation job you're always going to come across something you don't expect that will need fixing,' he said. 'And to allow extra time for unexpected delays as well. Even if you've had a survey done first, you're bound to come across something that will affect your schedule.'

'If the building is structurally sound, then I want the cinema up and running in eight weeks.'

'Eight weeks?' He looked shocked. 'Isn't that a bit fast?'

'It's the start of the school holidays,' she said. 'And it's always good to have a goal to work towards rather than being vague about things. That way you can plan and actually accomplish something instead of delivering nothing but hot air.'

'True.' He blew out a breath. 'But eight weeks is a big ask. Even if the place is structurally sound, it needs complete redecoration, you've got to sort out the fixtures and fittings, and there's no way you'll be able to do anything at all with the upstairs room until the ceiling's been sorted, not with that lead paint.' He frowned. 'I was thinking, that's probably why your grandfather used it as a storage room.'

'Because it would be too expensive to fix it, or it would take too much time?'

'Either or both,' he said. 'Just bear in mind you might not be able to have the whole building up and running at once. You might have to scale back to something more doable—say, start with the downstairs screen and kiosk refreshments only.'

Which would mean a lower income. And Nicole needed the place to make a decent profit, because she knew now that she really didn't want to go back to the bank. She wasn't afraid of hard work or long hours; she'd do whatever it took to make a go of the Electric Palace. But now she wanted to put the hours in for herself, not for a corporation that barely knew her name. 'I'm opening in eight weeks,' she said stubbornly.

'Where's your list of surveyors?' he asked.

'Here.' She flicked into the notes app on her phone and handed it to him.

He looked through the list. 'The first one's good, the second will cancel on you half a dozen times because he always overbooks himself, and the third is fine. I always like to get three quotes, so do you want the name of the guy I use, to replace the one who won't make it?'

'I'm eating humble pie already, aren't I?' she pointed out.

'Strictly speaking, you're eating a dark chocolate brownie,' he said, 'which you paid for. So no.' He sighed. 'OK. Would you have let Clarence help?'

She nodded.

'Say it out loud,' he said.

She would've done the same and made him admit it aloud, too. She gave in. 'Yes. I would've accepted help from Clarence.'

'Well, then. I thought we agreed at dinner that we're not on opposite sides?'

'We didn't really agree anything.'

'Hmm.' He added a set of contact details to her list and handed the phone back. 'I'd say from your old job that you'd be good at summing people up. Talk to all of them and go with the one your instinct tells you is right for the job.'

He wasn't pushing his guy first? So maybe he really was fair, rather than ruthless. Maybe she could trust him. 'Thank you,' she said.

'Pleasure.' He paused. 'What about builders?'

'I was going to ask the surveyor for recommendations.'

'That's a good idea.' He looked her straight in the eye. 'Though, again, I can give you contact details if you'd like them. I know you don't want to feel as if you owe me anything, but a recommendation from someone you know is worth a dozen testimonials from people you don't.'

'True.'

'And I wouldn't give you the name of someone who was unreliable or slapdash. Because that would affect my reputation,' he said.

She believed him. At least, on a business footing. Any other trust was out of her ability, right now.

'While you're here, do you want to see round the place?' he asked.

'You're going to give me a tour of the hotel?'

'Fair's fair—I made you give me a tour of the cinema,' he pointed out.

She smiled. 'That would be nice.'

The walls were made of the same mellow honey-coloured brick as her flat. She noticed that the ceilings of the rooms were all high.

'So this was an industrial complex before?' she asked.

'It was a spice warehouse,' he said, 'so we're naming all the function rooms accordingly. Cinnamon, coriander, caraway…'

'Sticking to the Cs?'

He laughed. 'I was thinking about maybe using a different letter on each floor. And I'm toying with "The Spice House" as our hotel name.'

'That might get you mixed up with a culinary supplier or an Indian restaurant,' she said.

'I'm still thinking about it,' he said.

'So this is a business hotel?'

One without the exclusive parking they'd planned originally. Instead, next door would be the cinema. And if Nicole would agree to keep the upper room as a flexible space and not just a fixed second screen, maybe there was a way they could work together. Something for the leisure side and not just the conference stuff she'd resisted earlier. Something that also might make his father finally see that Gabriel had vision and could be trusted with the future direction of the business.

'Business and leisure, mixed,' he said. 'We'll have a hundred and twenty-five bedrooms—that's twenty-five per floor on the top five floors—plus conference facilities on the first floor. We'll have meeting rooms with all the communications and connections our clients need, and a breakout area for networking or receptions. I want to be able to offer my clients everything from training and team-building events through to seminars and product launches. That's on the business side. On the leisure side, we can offer wedding receptions. I'm getting a licence so we can hold civil ceremonies here, too.' He paused. 'Though I've been thinking. Maybe you should be the one to get the wedding licence.'

'Me?' She looked surprised. 'You think people would want to get married in a cinema?'

'They'd want to get married in your upstairs room, especially if you're going to do the ceiling the way you described it to me,' he said. 'And that sweeping staircase would look amazing in wedding photos. The bride and groom, with the train of the bride's dress spread out over the stairs, or all the guests lined up on the stairs and leaning on that wrought iron banister—which would look great painted gold to match the stars on the ceiling.'

'So they'd have the wedding at the cinema, then go next door to you for the reception?'

'For the meal, yes. And then the upper room could turn back into a ballroom, if you wanted, with the bar next door or a temporary bar set up from the hotel if that's easier. Between us, we'd be able to offer a complete wedding package. The hotel has a honeymoon suite with a modern four-poster, and a health club and spa so we can offer beauty treatments. The morning of the wedding, we could do hair and make-up for the bride, attendants and anyone else in the wedding party. And maybe we could have a special movie screening, the next morning—something for the kids in the wedding party, perhaps?'

Working together.

Could it really be that easy?

'It's a possibility,' she said. 'But I want to think about it before I make any decision.'

'Fair enough.'

'So what else is in your health club and spa, apart from a hairdresser and beautician?'

'A heated pool, a gym with optional personal training packages, a sauna, steam room and whirlpool bath.' He ticked them off on his fingers. 'It's open to non-residents, like our restaurant.'

'And, being The Spice House, you'll specialise in spicy food?'

'Not necessarily, though we might have themed specials.' He smiled. 'The food will be locally sourced as far as possible, with seasonal menus. So far, it's all pretty standard stuff and I'd like to be able to offer our clients something a bit different, too, but I need to sit down and think about it.'

'If you want to brainstorm,' she said, 'and you

want to bounce ideas off—well, your neighbour…' The words were out before she could stop them.

'I'd like that,' he said. 'We came up with some good stuff between us about the cinema. And we've barely scratched the surface there.'

Georgygirl and Clarence. Their old friendship, which was in abeyance right now while she got her head round the fact that her friend was actually her business rival.

Could they transfer that friendship to a working relationship?

It would mean trusting him.

Baby steps, she reminded herself. She just needed to spend a little more time with him. Work out if he really was the same in real life as he'd been privately with her online.

He showed her round the rest of the hotel, then introduced her to his site manager. 'If anything crops up next door,' he said, 'come and see Ray.'

'If I don't know the answer myself,' Ray said, 'I'll know someone who does and can help sort it out for you.'

'Thank you,' she said, shaking Ray's hand and

liking how his handshake was firm without being overbearing.

Gabriel walked her to the door. 'Well, good luck with the surveyors and what have you. Let me know how you get on.'

'I will.'

For a moment, she thought he was going to lean forward and kiss her, and her heart actually skipped a beat.

But instead he held out his hand to shake hers.

Her skin tingled where he touched her. And she didn't dare look him in the eye, because she didn't want him to know what kind of effect he had on her. Besides, hadn't Jeff's mistress called her a cold fish? And Gabriel had dated a lot of women. Beautiful women. Passionate women. Way, way out of her league. Her confidence sank that little bit more.

'See you later,' she muttered, and fled.

When Nicole spoke to the surveyors, she found that Gabriel had been right on the money. The first one was booked up for the next few weeks, the second agreed to drop round that afternoon but then texted her half an hour later to cancel, the third could make it the following week, and the guy that Gabriel had recommended was able to see her first thing the next morning. Better still, he promised to have the report ready by the end of business that day.

It suited her timescale, but Nicole had the distinct feeling that Gabriel had called in a favour or two on her behalf. She couldn't exactly ask the surveyor if that was the case, and she felt it'd be mean-spirited to ask Gabriel himself—it would sound accusatory rather than grateful.

But there was something she could do.

She texted him.

Hey. You busy tomorrow night?

Why?

She really hoped this sounded casual.

Thought I could buy you dinner.

Absolutely not. I still owe you dinner.

But this is dinner with strings.

Ah. Dinner with strings?

She backed off.

OK. Sorry I asked.

Gabriel looked at the text and sighed. He hadn't meant to sound snippy at all. He'd been teasing her. That was the thing about texting: you couldn't pick up the tone.

He flicked into his contacts screen and called her. 'What are the strings, Nicole?'

'Builder names,' she said.

'You don't have to buy me dinner for that.'

'Yes, I do.'

Was this Nicole's way of saying she wanted to spend time with him but without admitting it? he wondered. But he knew he was just as bad. He wanted to spend time with her, too, but didn't want to admit it to her. 'Dinner would be fine. What time?'

'Seven? I thought maybe we could go to the pizza place just down from the café in Challoner Road. Meet you there?'

'Fine. Want a lift?'

'I'll meet you there,' she repeated.

Nicole and her over-developed sense of independence, he thought with an inward sigh. 'OK. See you at seven.'

She was already there waiting for him when he walked into the pizzeria at precisely one minute to seven, the next evening. She was wearing a pretty, summery dress and he was tempted to tell her how nice she looked, but he didn't want to make her back away. Instead, he asked, 'How did the survey go?'

'Remarkably quickly. Considering that normally people are booked up for at least a week in advance, and it takes several days to do a survey report, it's amazing that your guy not only managed to fit me in this morning,' she said, 'he also emailed me the report at the close of business this afternoon.'

Oh. So she'd picked up the fact that he'd called in a favour. Well, of course she would. She was bright. 'Remarkable,' he said coolly.

'*Incredibly* remarkable,' she said, 'which is why I'm buying you dinner to say thank you for whatever favours you called in on my behalf. And I've already given the waiter my card, so you can't—'

He laughed, and she stopped. 'What?'

'You're such a control freak,' he said.

'No, I'm not.' She folded her arms in the classic defensive posture. 'I just don't want to—'

'—be beholden to me,' he finished. 'Is that what your ex did?'

She flushed. 'I don't know what you're talking about.'

Something had made her super-independent, and he had a feeling that there was a man involved. A man who'd broken her trust so she didn't date any more? 'Everything came with strings?' he asked softly.

'No. I just pay my own way, that's all. Right now, I feel I owe you. And I'm not comfortable owing you.'

'Friends don't owe each other for helping,' he said gently. Perhaps it was mean of him, using insider knowledge of her family and closest friends, but how else was he going to make Nicole understand that this was OK? 'Do you insist on going halves with your mum or Jessie? Or work a strict rotation on whose turn it is to buy coffee?'

'No,' she admitted. 'And how do you know about Jessie? Is your dossier that big?'

'No. You told me about your best friend when we were talking late one night, Georgy,' he reminded her. 'And I happen to have a good memory.'

She sighed. 'I guess. Can we go back to talking about surveyors?'

'Because it's safe?'

She gave him a speaking look. 'We ought to look at the menu. They'll be over in a minute to take our order.'

Was she running scared because this felt like a date? Or was the wariness specific to him? He decided to let her off the hook. For now. 'We don't need to look at the menu. I already know you're going to order a margherita with an avocado and rocket salad,' he said instead.

She looked at him. 'And you'll pick a quattro formaggi with a tomato and basil salad.'

He could swear she'd just been about to call him 'Clarence'.

And this was what he'd fantasised about when he'd messaged her over the last few months. Going on a date just like this, where they'd talk about anything and everything and knew each other so well that they could finish each other's sentences.

Except this wasn't a date. She'd called it dinner with strings. Because she felt beholden to him. And he didn't quite know how to sort this out.

'Dough balls first?' he suggested.

'Definitely.' She looked at him. 'This is weird.'

'What is?'

'We know each other. And at the same time we don't.'

'More do than don't,' he said. But he could tell that something was holding her back. Someone, he guessed, who'd hurt her. Was that why she found it hard to trust him? The one topic they'd always shied away from was relationships. He'd stopped dating because he only seemed to attract the kind of women who wanted someone else to fund a flashy lifestyle for them, and he was tired of the superficiality. Though he knew without having to ask that Nicole wouldn't discuss whatever was holding her back. He'd just have to persuade her to tell him. Little by little.

The waiter came to take their order, breaking that little bit of awkwardness.

And then Nicole went back into business mode. 'Builders,' she said, and handed him her phone.

He looked at her list. 'They're all fine,' he said. 'It's a matter of when they can fit you in. If you get stuck, I can give you some more names.'

'Thank you.'

'So how was the survey?' he asked. 'Is there much structural stuff to do?'

'A small amount of rewiring, a damp patch that needs further investigation, a bit of work to the windows, doing what you already said to the upstairs room ceiling, and then the rest of it's cosmetic.'

'Even if you can get a builder to start straight away,' he said, 'it's still going to take a fair bit of time to do all the cosmetic stuff. If you renovate the seats in the auditorium, it'll take a while; and if you rip them out completely and replace them with the sofas you were talking about, you'll have work to do on the flooring. And there's the cost to think about. Doing something in a shorter timescale means paying overtime or getting in extra staff—all of which costs and it'll blow your budget.'

She raised her eyebrows. 'You're telling an ex-banker to keep an eye on the budget?'

He smiled. 'I know that's ironic—but you've fallen in love with the building, and there's a danger that could blind you to the cost.'

'I guess.'

'It is—'

'—what it is,' she finished with a wry smile.

The waiter brought the dough balls and the garlic butter to dip them into, and they focused on that for a moment—but then Gabriel's fingers brushed against Nicole's when they both reached for a dough ball at the same time.

It felt like an electric shock.

He hadn't been this aware of anyone in a long, long time. And he really didn't know what to do about it. If he pushed too hard, she'd back away. If he played it cool, she'd think he wasn't interested.

This felt like being eighteen again, totally unsure of himself—and Gabriel was used to knowing what he was doing and what his next move would be.

The only safe topic of conversation was the cinema. And even that was a minefield, because she'd backed off every time he'd suggested working together.

'There is one way to get a bigger workforce without massive costs,' he said.

She frowned. 'How?'

'Remember that group on the Surrey Quays forum who said they wanted the cinema up and running again? I bet they'd offer to help.'

She shook her head. Her mother had suggested the same thing, but it felt wrong. 'I can't ask people to work for me for nothing.'

'You can if it's a community thing,' he said. 'They're interested in the building. So let them be involved in the restoration. If they don't have the expertise themselves, they'll probably know someone who does. And any retired French polisher would take a look at that counter-top in your foyer and itch to get his or her hands on it.'

'Nice save, with the "or her",' she said dryly.

'I'm not sexist. Being good at your job has nothing to do with your gender,' he pointed out.

'It still feels wrong to ask people to work for free.'

'What about if you give them a public acknowledgement? You could have a plaque on the wall in the foyer with the names of everyone who's been involved.'

'I like that idea,' she said slowly. 'And they're my target audience, so it makes sense to talk to them about what I'm doing—to see whether they'd be prepared to support it and see a movie at the Electric Palace rather than going into the West End.'

'You want their views on the programming, you mean?' he asked.

She nodded. 'If I show any of say the top three blockbusters, I'll have to pay the film distributors at least half the box office receipts,' she said. 'And I'll be competing with the multiplexes—which we both know I can't do effectively.'

'So what's the alternative? Art-house or local film-makers? Because that'd mean a smaller potential audience.'

'I need to find the right mix of commercial films, regional and art-house,' she said. 'Maybe I need to run it as a cinema club.'

'That might limit your audience, though,' he said. 'You could always put some polls up on the Surrey Quays website to see what kind of thing people want to see and when. And think about a loyalty scheme. Buy ten tickets and get a free coffee, that sort of thing.'

'It's a thought.'

He could tell she was backing off again, so he kept the conversation light for the rest of their meal.

'Thank you for dinner,' he said. 'Can I walk you home?'

'I live in the opposite direction to you,' she reminded him.

He shrugged. 'The walk will do me good.'

'Then, put that way, OK.'

His hand brushed against hers on the way back to her flat, and he had to suppress the urge to curl his fingers round hers. They weren't dating.

And it was even harder to stop himself kissing her goodnight. Her mouth looked so soft, so sweet. He itched to find out how her mouth would feel against his.

But this wasn't appropriate. If he did what he really wanted to do, she'd run a mile. He took a step back. 'Well. Goodnight. And thank you again for dinner.'

'Thank you for the advice and the brainstorming,' she said, equally politely.

'Any time.' He smiled, and turned away before he did anything stupid. She still wasn't having those late-night conversations with him like they used to have. And until they'd got that easiness back, he needed to keep his distance.

The more he got to know her, the more he wanted to know her. He *liked* her. But she clearly didn't feel the same way about him.

It is what it is, he reminded himself.

Even though he really wanted to change things.

CHAPTER SEVEN

ONLY ONE OF the builders on Nicole's list could actually come to look at the cinema within the next couple of days. One was too busy to come at all and the third couldn't make it for another month. She'd already cleared out as much junk as she could from the cinema so, until she'd seen the builder's quote and agreed the terms of business, Nicole knew she couldn't do much more at the cinema. All the paperwork was up to date, too, and she was simply waiting on replies. To keep herself busy instead of fretting about the downtime, she headed for the archives.

There were newspaper reports of the opening of the Kursaal in 1911, but to her disappointment there were no photographs. There was a brief description of the outside of the building, including the arch outside which apparently had Art Deco sun rays in the brickwork, but nothing about the ceiling of stars. She carefully typed out the relevant paragraphs—the font size was too small to be easily read on a photograph—and was about to give up looking when the archivist came to see her.

'You might like to have a look through this,' she said, handing Nicole a thick album. 'They're postcards of the area, from around the early nineteen hundreds. There might be something in there.'

'Thank you,' Nicole said. 'If there is, can I take a photograph on my phone?'

'As long as you don't use flash. And if I can think of any other sources which might contain something about the cinema, I'll bring them over,' the archivist said.

Halfway through the postcard album, Nicole found a postcard of the Electric Palace; she knew that, in common with other similarly named buildings, its name had changed after the First World War, to make it sound less German. Clearly by then someone had painted the outside of the building white, because the sun rays on the arch had been covered over, as they were now.

She photographed the postcard carefully, then slipped the postcard from the little corners keeping it in place so she could read the back. The frank on the stamp told her that the card had been posted in 1934. To her delight, the inscription referred to the writer spending the previous night dancing in the ballroom—and also to seeing the film *It Happened One Night*, the previous week.

Clarence would be pleased to know there was a reference to Frank Capra, she thought as she carefully photographed the inscription.

Gabriel, she corrected herself.

And that was the problem. She really wanted to share this with Gabriel. Yet she already knew how rubbish her judgement was in men. Getting close to Gabriel Hunter would be a huge mistake.

Then again, the man she was getting to know was a decent man. Maybe he wouldn't let her down. Or maybe he would. So it would be sensible to keep it strictly business between them. Even though she was beginning to want a lot more than that.

* * *

On Saturday night, Nicole was sitting on her own in her flat. Usually by now on a Saturday she'd be talking to Clarence online, but she hadn't messaged him since she'd found out who he really was. She hadn't spent much time on the Surrey Quays website, either; it had felt awkward. Nobody had sent her a direct message, so clearly she hadn't been missed.

Nobody had been in touch from the bank, either, to see how things were going. It had been stupid to think that the last leaving drink had been a kind of new beginning; she was most definitely out of sight and out of mind. Her best friend was away for the weekend and so was her mother, which left her pretty much on her own.

She flicked through a few channels on the television. There was nothing on that she wanted to watch. Maybe she ought to analyse her competitors and start researching cinema programming, but right at that moment she felt lonely and miserable and wished she had someone to share it with. Which was weak, feeble and totally pathetic, she told herself.

Though she might as well admit it: she missed Clarence.

Did Gabriel miss Georgygirl? she wondered.

And now she was being *really* feeble. 'Get over it, Nicole,' she told herself crossly.

She spent a while looking up the programming in various other small cinemas, to give herself a few ideas, and then her phone rang. She glanced at the screen: Gabriel. So he'd been thinking of her? Pleasure flooded through her.

Though it was probably a business call. Which was how it ought to be, and she should respond accordingly. *Sensibly.* She answered the phone. 'Good evening, Gabriel,' she said coolly.

'Good evening, Nicole. Are you busy tomorrow?' he asked.

'It's Sunday tomorrow,' she prevaricated, not wanting to admit to him that her social life was a complete desert.

'I know. But, if you're free, I'd like to take you on a research trip tomorrow.'

'Research trip?' Was this his way of asking her out without making it sound like a date? Her heart skipped a beat.

'To see a ceiling.'

Oh. So he really did mean just business. She did her best to suppress the disappointment. 'Where?'

'Norfolk.'

'Isn't that a couple of hours' drive away?'

'This particular bit is about two and a half hours away,' he said. 'I'll pick you up at nine tomorrow morning. Wear shorts, or jeans you can roll up to your knees, and flat shoes you can take off easily. Oh, and a hat.'

'What sort of hat?'

'Whatever keeps the sun off.'

'Why? And why do I need to take my shoes off?'

'You'll see when you get there.' And then, annoyingly, he rang off before she could ask anything else.

Shorts, a hat and flat shoes.

What did that have to do with a ceiling?

She was none the wiser when Gabriel rang the intercom to her flat, the next morning.

'I'm on my way down,' she said.

'You look nice,' he said, smiling at her when

she opened the main door to the flats. 'That's the first time I've ever seen your hair loose.'

To her horror, Nicole could feel herself blushing at the compliment. Oh, for pity's sake. She was twenty-eight, not fifteen. 'Thanks,' she mumbled. It didn't help that he was wearing faded denims and a T-shirt and he looked really *touchable*. Her fingertips actually tingled with the urge to reach out and see how soft the denim was.

And then he reached out and twirled the end of her hair round his fingers. Just briefly. 'Like silk,' he said.

She couldn't look him in the eye. She didn't want him to know that she felt as if her knees had just turned to sand. 'So what's this ceiling?' she asked.

'Tin. Like the cinema. Except restored.'

'And you know about it because...?'

'I've seen it before,' he said, and ushered her over to his car. 'This is why I said you need a hat, by the way.'

'Show-off,' she said as he put the roof of his convertible down.

He spread his hands. 'There aren't that many

days in an English spring or summer when you can enjoy having the roof down. This is one of them. Got your hat?'

She grabbed the baseball cap from her bag and jammed it onto her head. 'Happy?'

'Happy. You can drive, if you want,' he said, surprising her.

She blinked. 'You'd actually trust me to drive this?'

'It's insured,' he said, 'and I know where we're going, so I can direct you.'

'I don't have a car,' she said. 'I use public transport most of the time. The only time I drive is if there's a team thing at work and I have a pool car. That doesn't happen very often.'

'But you have a licence and you can drive.' He handed her the car keys. 'Here. Knock yourself out.'

'Why?'

'Because it'll distract you and stop you asking me questions,' he said. 'And also because I think you might enjoy it. This car's a lot of fun to drive.'

He trusted her.

Maybe she needed to do the same for him.

'Thank you,' she said.

Gabriel's directions were perfect—given clearly and in plenty of time—and Nicole discovered that he was right. His car really was fun to drive. And it was the perfect day for driving a convertible, with the sun out and the lightest of breezes. Once they were on the motorway heading northeast from London, Gabriel switched the radio to a station playing retro nineties music, and she found herself singing along with him.

She couldn't remember the last time she'd enjoyed herself so much.

'Want to pull into the next lay-by and swap over?' he asked. 'Then you can just enjoy the scenery instead of concentrating on directions and worrying that you're going to take the wrong exit off a roundabout.'

'OK.'

They drove along the coast road, and she discovered that he was right; it really was gorgeous scenery.

'They found that famous hoard of Iron Age gold torcs near here, at Snettisham,' he said.

'Is that where we're going?'

'No.'

Annoyingly, he wouldn't tell her any more until he pulled in to a hotel car park.

'The Staithe Hotel,' she said, reading the sign. 'Would this place have the ceiling we're coming to see?'

'It would indeed.'

'Staithe?'

'It's an Old English word meaning "riverbank" or "landing stage",' he said. 'You see it mainly nowadays in place names in east and north-east England—the bits that were under Danelaw.'

Clearly he'd done his research. Years ago, maybe there had been some kind of wharf here. 'Are we dressed suitably for a visit?' she asked doubtfully. 'It looks quite posh.'

'We're fine.'

Then she twigged. 'It's *yours*, isn't it?'

'The first hotel I worked on by myself,' he confirmed. 'It was pretty run-down and Dad wasn't entirely sure I was doing the right thing, when I bid for it at the auction, but I really liked the place. And the views are stunning.'

When they went in, the receptionist greeted them warmly. 'Have you booked a table?' she asked.

'No, but I'd like to see the manager—he's expecting me,' Gabriel said.

'Just a moment, sir,' the receptionist said, and disappeared into the room behind the reception desk.

The manager came out and smiled when he saw them. 'Gabriel, it's good to see you.' He shook Gabriel's hand warmly.

'You, too. Pete, this is my friend Nicole Thomas,' Gabriel said.

Friend. The word made her feel warm inside. Were they friends, now?

'Nicole, this is Pete Baines, my manager here.'

'Pleased to meet you, Mr Baines.' She shook his hand.

'Call me Pete,' the manager said. 'Any friend of Gabriel's is a friend of mine.'

'Nicole is renovating the cinema next door to the place I'm working on at the moment,' Gabriel explained, 'and her ceiling has a lot in common with the one in your restaurant.'

'I get you,' Pete said. 'Come with me, Nicole.' He ushered her into the restaurant.

The ceiling looked like elaborate plasterwork, as did the wainscoting around the fireplace.

'Believe it or not, that's tin, not carving or plaster,' Pete said. 'It's just painted to look that way. Obviously Gabriel knows a lot more than I do on that front—I just run the place and boss everyone about.'

'And very well, too. Pete, I know you're normally booked out weeks ahead,' Gabriel said.

'But you want me to squeeze you in for lunch?' Pete finished, smiling. 'I'm sure we can do something.'

'Any chance of a table on the terrace, outside?' Gabriel asked.

'Sure. I'll leave you to take a closer look at the ceiling. Can I get you both a drink?'

'Sparkling mineral water for me, please,' Nicole said.

'Make that two,' Gabriel added.

'I can't believe this isn't plasterwork,' Nicole said, looking at the ceiling and wainscoting.

'It's tin. The place was originally built in Victorian times by a local businessman. His son remodelled it to make the room look more Tudor and added the tin wainscoting and ceiling.' He flicked into his phone. 'This is what it looked like before the restoration.'

She looked at the photographs. 'It looks a mess, there—but you can't see any of the damage here.' She gestured to the wainscoting in front of her.

'I can let you have the restoration guy's name, if you'd like it. And, by the way, as you paid at La Chiatta, I'm buying lunch here. No arguments,' he said. 'Otherwise you'll just have to starve.'

'Noted,' she said. 'And thank you.'

When they sat out on the terrace and she'd read the menu, she looked at Gabriel. 'This menu's amazing. Is all the food locally sourced?' she asked.

'Yes. The locals love us, and we've had some good write-ups in the national papers as well—Pete gets foodies coming all the way from London to stay for the weekend. The chef's great and we're hoping to get a Michelin star in the next round,' Gabriel said.

'What do you recommend?'

'Start from the puddings and work backwards,' he said.

She looked at the dessert menu and smiled. 'I think I know what I'm having.'

'White chocolate and raspberry bread and butter pudding?' he asked.

At her nod, he grinned. 'Me, too.'

'Crab salad for mains, then,' she said.

'Share some sweet potato fries?' he suggested.

This felt much more like a date than the other times they'd eaten together—even though they'd officially come on a research trip to look at the tin ceiling.

The view from the terrace was really pretty across the salt marshes and then to the sea. 'I can't believe how far the sand stretches,' she said.

'That's why I said wear shoes you can take off and jeans you can roll up,' he said. 'We're going for a walk on the beach after lunch to work off the calories from the pudding, and to blow the cobwebs out.'

'I can't actually remember the last time I went to the beach,' she said.

'Me, neither. I really love this part of the coast.

When the tide's out you can walk for miles across the sand, and you've got the seal colony just down the road at Blakeney.'

'You fell in love with Norfolk when you worked on the hotel, didn't you?' she asked.

'I very nearly ended up moving here,' he said, 'but London suits me better.'

'So is that your big dream? Living by the sea?'

'I love the sea, but I'm happy where I am,' he said.

She enjoyed the food, which was beautifully presented and tasted even better than it looked. Though her fingers brushed against his a couple of times when they shared the sweet potato fries, and her skin tingled where he'd touched her.

To distract herself, she said, 'There was something I wanted to show you yesterday. I found something in the archives.' She found the photographs she'd taken and handed her phone to him.

He looked at the front of the postcard, zoomed in on the script, and smiled. 'Well, how about that—a photograph of someone who danced there and saw a Capra film.'

'I thought of you,' she said. 'With the Capra stuff.'

'What a fantastic find.'

'There was a newspaper article, too.' She took the phone back to find her notes for him. 'The print's so tiny that a photograph wouldn't have helped, so I took notes. The outside of the building wasn't originally all white, and there's a sun ray on that semi-circle. Do you think I could get that back?'

'You need to talk to the builder—it depends on the condition of the brickwork underneath. But it's a possibility.' He gave her another of those knee-melting smiles. 'This is amazing. A real connection to the past. Thanks for sharing this with me.'

She almost told him that he was the one person she'd really wanted to share it with; but she knew he saw this as just business, so she'd be sensible and keep it light between them. 'I did look to see if there was a photograph of the warehouse in that scrapbook, but I'm afraid there wasn't anything.'

'I doubt there would be postcards of the warehouse.' He shrugged. 'People didn't really pay that much attention to industrial buildings, except for things like train stations and museums.'

Once they'd said goodbye to Pete, Gabriel drove a little way down the road to the car park.

'Good—the tide's out,' he said.

'How do you know?'

'Because the car park's dry—I learned that one the hard way,' he said with a grin, 'though fortunately not in this car.'

Once they'd parked, he took a bag from the boot of the car.

'What's that?'

'Something we need to do, Georgy.'

Obviously he wasn't going to tell her until he was ready, so she let it go. She took her shoes off at the edge of the beach, as did he. As she walked along with her shoes in one hand, her other hand brushed against his a couple of times, and every single nerve-end was aware of him. With a partner, she thought, this place would be so romantic. But Gabriel wasn't her partner. Romance wasn't in the equation, not with Gabriel and not with anyone else.

'Is that a wreck out there?' she asked.

'Yes. It's not a good idea to walk out to it, though, as when the tide changes it comes in really quickly. And it comes in far enough to flood the road to the car park.' He stopped. 'Here will do nicely.'

'For what?'

'This.' He took a kite from the bag.

She burst out laughing. Now she understood why he'd called her Georgy again. 'I've never flown a kite before,' she reminded him.

'It's been a while for me,' he admitted. 'But this is the perfect place to start.'

'The wind's blowing my hair into my eyes. I need to tie my hair back,' she said, flustered. The idea of intense businessman Gabriel Hunter being carefree was something she found it hard to get her head around. She wasn't the carefree sort, either. But she was a different person when she was with him—Georgygirl. Just as she had a feeling that he was different when he was with her.

He waited while she put an elastic hairband in her hair, then handed her the kite. 'Stand with your back to the wind, hold the kite up, let out the line a little, and it will lift. Then you pull on the line so it climbs.'

She couldn't get the hang of it and the kite nose-dived into the sand again and again. 'I'd better let you have this back before I wreck it,' she said eventually.

'No. Try it like this,' he said, and stood behind her with his hands over hers, guiding her so that the kite actually went up into the air, this time. He felt warm and strong, and Nicole couldn't help leaning back into him.

He tensed for a moment; then he wrapped one arm round her waist, holding her close to him.

Neither of them said a word, just concentrated on flying the kite; but Nicole was so aware of Gabriel's cheek pressed against hers, the warmth of his skin and the tiny prickle of new stubble. She could feel his heart beating against her back, firm and steady, and she was sure he could probably feel her own heart racing. Taking a risk, she laid her arm over his, curling her hand round his elbow.

They stood there for what felt like for ever, just holding each other close.

Then he slowly wound the kite in and dropped it on the sand, and twisted her round to face him.

'Nicole,' he said, and his eyes were very bright.

She couldn't help looking at his mouth.

And then he dipped his head and brushed his mouth against hers. So soft, so sweet, so gentle.

It felt as if someone had lit touch-paper inside her.

She slid her arms round his neck, drawing him closer, and let him deepen the kiss. Then she closed her eyes and completely lost herself in the way he made her feel, the warmth of his mouth moving against hers, the way he was holding her.

And then he broke the kiss.

'Nicole.' His voice was huskier, deeper. 'I'm sorry. I shouldn't have done that.'

'Neither should I.' What an idiot she'd been. Had she learned nothing from Jeff? She was a cold fish, useless at relationships.

'I… Maybe we need to get back to London,' he said.

She seized on the excuse gratefully. 'Yes. I have a lot to do for the cinema and I'm sure you're busy, too.'

* * *

No. He wasn't. He could delegate every single thing that he had on his desk for the next month and spend all his time with her.

That was what he wanted to do.

But that kiss had been a mistake. She'd backed away from him. He'd taken it too far, too fast and he knew he needed to let her regroup. He'd let himself be carried away by the fun of kite-flying. Acted on impulse. Blown it.

They walked back to the car, and he was careful this time not to let his hand brush against hers. And he kept the roof up in the car on the way back.

'No wind in your hair this time?' she asked.

He shrugged. 'It is what it is.'

'Why do you always say that?'

'It's something Vijay taught me. If you're in a situation and you can't change it, you need to accept that and make the best of it. Don't waste your energy in trying to change something that you can't change; focus instead on what you can do.'

'It's a good philosophy.'

He smiled. 'I would say it's very Zen—except he's a Hindu, not a Buddhist.'

Nicole had a feeling that Gabriel had been very lonely when he grew up and the Khans had been the first ones to make him really feel part of the family; whereas she'd always grown up knowing she was loved, by her mother and her godparents and the rest of her mother's friends. It didn't matter that she didn't have a big family by blood, or that her father had been a liar and a cheat, or that her grandparents were estranged.

She wondered how she'd moved from that to her place at the bank, where she'd never really been part of the team and had only really felt accepted on her very last day there.

It is what it is.

She couldn't change the past: but she could change her future.

So, when Gabriel parked outside her flat, she turned to face him. 'Would you like to come in for coffee?'

* * *

'Coffee?' Gabriel stared at her. 'Is that a good idea?'

'You're not a predator, Gabriel.'

'Thank you for that.' So maybe she'd forgiven him for that kiss?

'Come and have coffee,' she said.

'OK. That'd be nice.' He followed her upstairs to her first-floor flat. The front door opened into a small lobby with five doors leading off. 'Storage cupboard, bathroom, kitchen, living room, bedroom,' she said, indicating the doors in turn. 'Do go and sit down.'

The walls in her living room were painted a pale primrose-yellow, and the floors were polished wood with a blue patterned rug in the centre. French doors at the far end of the room led onto a small balcony, and just in front of them was a glass-topped bistro table with two chairs. He was half surprised not to see a desk in the room, but assumed that was probably in her bedroom—not that he was going to ask. There were a couple of fairly anonymous framed prints on the walls, and on the mantelpiece there were a couple of framed photographs. The older woman with Nicole looked so much like her that Gabriel realised straight away she had to be Nicole's mother; the younger woman in the other photograph was wearing a bridal dress and Nicole appeared to be wearing a bridesmaid's outfit, so he assumed this was her best friend Jessie.

Looking at the photos felt a bit like spying; and he felt too awkward to sit on the sofa. In the end, he went through to the kitchen—which was as tidy and neat as her living room.

'Can I help?' he asked.

'No, you're fine. Do you want a sandwich or anything?'

He shook his head. What he really wanted was to be back on that beach with her in his arms, kissing him back. But that was a subject that could really blow up in his face. He needed to take this carefully. 'Thanks, but just coffee will do me.'

'Here.' She handed him a mug, and ushered him back into the living room. She took her laptop from a drawer and said, 'I was going to put a note on the Surrey Quays website tonight. As you're part of it, too, I thought maybe we could do this together.'

Was she suggesting that he told everyone who he was? He looked warily at her. 'I kind of like my anonymity there.'

'So be Clarence. You don't have to tell them you're Gabriel.'

'Are you going to out yourself?' he asked.

'I kind of have to, given that I've inherited the Electric Palace—but I think everyone's going to respond to me as Georgygirl. Nobody knows Nicole the banker.'

But was she Nicole, Georgy, or a mixture of the two? And could she drop the protective shell of being the hard-headed banker and become the woman he thought she really was? Because, with her, he found that he was the man he wanted to be. Not the one who kept his tongue bitten and seethed in silent frustration when he kept failing to earn his father's respect: the man who thought outside the box and saw the world in full colour.

She put her mug on the coffee table, signed into the Surrey Quays forum, and started to type.

'I guess "Electric Palace—news" is probably the best subject line to use,' she said.

'Probably,' he agreed.

She typed rapidly, then passed the laptop to him so he could see the screen properly. 'Do you think this will do?'

Sorry I've been AWOL for a bit. I've been getting my head round the fact that I'm the new owner of the Electric Palace—it was left to me in a will. It needs a bit of work, but my boss has given me a six-month sabbatical and I'm going to use it to see if I can get it up and running again.

I'm planning to start showing films in a couple of months—a mix of blockbusters, classics and art-house films, and maybe showcase the work of new local film-makers. I have a few ideas about what to do with the upper room—the old ballroom—and I really want it to be used as part of the community. If anyone's looking for a regular room for a dance class or teaching craft work or that sort of thing, give me a yell. And if anyone has photographs I can borrow to enlarge for the walls, I'd be really grateful.

Cheers, Georgygirl x

'So you're not going to ask for help restoring the place?' he asked.

She shook her head. 'That feels kind of greedy and rude.'

'There's a saying, shy bairns get naught,' he reminded her.

'And there's another saying, nobody likes pushy people. If people offer to help, that's a different thing.' She looked him straight in the eye. 'Someone fairly wise keeps telling me "it is what it is".'

'I guess.' He smiled. 'So what now?'

'We wait and see if anyone replies.'

'And you and me?' The question had to be asked. They couldn't keep pretending.

She sucked in a breath. 'I don't know. I've got a business to set up. I don't have time for a relationship. The same goes for you.'

'What if I think it's worth making time?'

She sighed. 'I'm not very good at relationships.'

'Neither am I.'

'So we ought to be sensible. Anyway, we're

business rivals, so we're both off limits to each other.'

'Not so much rivals as working together. Collaborating. The wedding stuff, for starters,' he reminded her.

'We haven't agreed that.'

'I know, but it's a win for both of us, Nicole. We both get what we want. And it doesn't matter whose idea it was in the first place. It works.'

'Maybe.'

But this time there was no coolness in her voice—she sounded unsure, but he didn't think it was because she didn't trust his judgement. It felt more as if she had no confidence in herself. Hadn't she just said she wasn't good at relationships?

'You kissed me back on the beach,' he said softly. 'I think that means something.'

She flushed. 'Temporary loss of sanity. That's what kite-flying does to you.'

'We're not flying kites now. And we're back in London.' He raised an eyebrow. 'What would you do if I kissed you again?'

'Panic,' she said.

She'd been straight with him. He couldn't ask for more than that. 'Thank you for being honest.' But he needed to be sure about this. 'Is it me, or is it all men?'

'I…' She shook her head. 'I'm just not good at relationships.'

He took her hand. 'He must have really hurt you.'

'He never hit me.'

'There's more than one way to hurt someone. It could be with words, or it could be by ignoring them, or it could be by undermining their self-esteem and constantly wanting to make them into someone they're not.'

'Leave it. Please.' Her eyes shimmered, and she blinked back the tears.

'I can't promise I won't hurt you, Nicole. But I can promise I'll try my very best not to hurt you. If I do, it definitely won't be deliberate.' He lifted her hand up to his mouth and kissed the back of her hand. 'I have no idea where this thing between us is going. And I'm not very good at relationships. But I like the way I feel when I'm with you.' He owed her some honesty, too. 'I didn't want to meet Georgygirl in case she wasn't the same in real life as she was online. I didn't want to be disappointed.'

She looked away. 'Uh-huh.'

Was that what her ex had said to her? That she disappointed him? 'When I met you, I thought you were this hard-headed businesswoman, cold and snooty.'

She still didn't meet his eyes or say a word.

'But,' he said softly, 'then I got to know you a bit better. And in real life you're the woman I've been talking to online, late at night. You're clever and you're funny and you sparkle. That's who you really are.'

This time, she looked at him. 'So are you the man I've been talking to? The one who's full of sensible advice, who makes me laugh and who seems to understand who I am?'

'I think so. Because I've been more myself with you than I've been with anyone. For years and years,' he said.

'This is a risk.'

'You took risks all the time at the bank. You're taking a risk now on the Electric Palace.'

'Those were all calculated risks,' she pointed out. 'This isn't something I can calculate.'

'Me, neither. But I like you, Nicole. I like you a lot. And I think if we're both brave we might just have the chance to have something really special.'

'I'm not sure how brave I am,' she admitted.

'It's harder to be brave on your own. But you're not on your own, Nicole. We're in this together.'

Could she believe him?

Could she trust him—and trust that he wouldn't let her down like Jeff had?

She thought about it.

Gabriel could've taken advantage of her in business. But he hadn't. He'd been scrupulously fair. Pushy, yes, but his ideas really did work for both of them.

He'd also completely fried her common sense with that kiss on the beach.

And she'd been honest about her life right now. She was going to be crazily busy with the cinema. She didn't have time for a relationship. It was the same for him, getting the hotel next door up and running.

But they could make the time.

'OK. We'll see how it goes. No promises, and we try not to hurt each other,' she said.

'Works for me.'

She looked at him. 'So does that mean you're going to kiss me now?'

'Nope.'

Had she got this wrong? Didn't he want a relationship with her after all? Confused, she stared at him.

'You're going to kiss me,' he said. 'And then I'm going to kiss you back.'

Could it really be that easy?

She's a cold fish.

Nicole shoved the thought away. She didn't feel like a cold fish with Gabriel. He made her blood heat.

Slowly, hoping that she was going to get this right, she leaned over and touched her mouth to the corner of his.

He made a small murmur of approval, and she grew braver, nibbling at his lower lip.

Then he wrapped his arms round her and opened his mouth, kissing her back.

And Nicole felt as if something had cracked in the region of her heart.

She wasn't sure how long they stayed there, just kissing, but eventually Gabriel stroked her face. 'Much as I'd like to scoop you up right now and carry you to your bed, I don't have any condoms on me.'

She felt her face flame. 'Neither do I.'

'I've dated a lot,' he said, 'but for the record I'm actually quite picky about who I sleep with. And it's not usually on a first date, either.'

'Is today our first date?'

'Maybe. Maybe not.' He stole another kiss. 'Can I see you tomorrow?'

'You work next door to me. The chances are we'll see each other.'

'Not work. After,' he corrected.

'A proper date?'

'Give me a while to think up something to impress you.'

'Clarence,' she pointed out, 'wouldn't try to impress me. He'd just be himself.'

'And if I tried to impress Georgy, she would probably be so sarcastic with me that I'd have a permanent hole in my self-esteem.' He stole another kiss. 'See what we feel like after work? Drink, dinner, or just a walk along the waterfront?'

'Sounds good to me.'

'Tomorrow,' he said. 'I'm going now while I still have a few shreds of common sense left.'

'OK. And thank you for today. For the kite and the ceiling and…everything.'

'I liked the kite. I haven't done that in years. Maybe we could do that again—say on Parliament Hill.' He kissed her one last time. 'See you tomorrow, Nicole.'

'See you tomorrow, Gabriel.' She saw him out.

Later that evening her phone pinged with a text from him.

Sweet dreams.

They would be, she thought. Because they'd be of him.

CHAPTER EIGHT

THE NEXT MORNING, Nicole came out of the shower to find a text from Gabriel on her phone.

Good morning :) x

She smiled and called him back. 'Don't tell me you're at work already.'

'No. I hit the gym first; it clears my head for the day. I'm walking to the hotel now. What are you doing today?'

'Talking to a builder.'

'Want some back-up?' he asked.

'Thanks for the offer, but I'm fine.'

'OK. But let me look at the quote—and the contract, when you get to that stage,' he said.

Her old suspicions started to rise, but quickly deflated when he added, 'I write contracts like this all the time, so it'll take me all of ten minutes to look over them. And my rates are good—I'll work for coffee and a brownie. Maybe a kiss.'

His candour disarmed her. 'OK. Thanks. Though I saw contracts all the time in my old job, too, you know,' she pointed out.

'I know, but you were more interested in cash-flow and gearing than anything else,' he said. 'I bet you can analyse a balance sheet in half the time that I do.'

'Says Mr MBA.'

'Yeah, well. Has anyone replied to your post, yet?'

'I don't know. Hang on a sec.' She switched on her laptop and flicked in to the site. 'Oh, my God.'

'Is everything OK?' He sounded concerned.

'There's… Gabriel, take a look for yourself. There are loads and loads and loads of replies. I can't believe this.' She scrolled through them. 'So many names I recognise, and they all want to be part of it. Some people are offering me photographs. A few want to come and have a look round, in exchange for putting a bit of paint on the walls. I've got someone who used to be a projectionist, and offers from people who want to be ushers, and there's a couple of people who say they can't manage going up a ladder or holding a paintbrush because their arthritis is too bad but they'll come and make tea for the task team and do fetching and carrying and stuff.' Tears pricked her eyes. 'I don't know if I'm more humbled or thrilled.'

'I'm not surprised you've had that kind of reaction,' he said.

'Why?'

'Because people like you,' he said. 'Your posts are always thoughtful and considered, and people respect you.'

People actually liked her? Nicole couldn't quite get her head round that. In real life, she'd tended to keep part of herself back, particularly since Jeff's betrayal; but online, behind her screen name, she'd been more who she really was.

Would they all change their minds about her when they met her? Gabriel hadn't. But the doubts still flickered through her.

'I think,' he said, 'I take it back about it being a big ask to be open in July. I think you're going to do it, Nicole, because you've got the whole community behind you. Including me.'

'Thank you.'

'Good luck with your builder. Call me if you need back-up.'

'I will.' She had no intention of doing so, but she appreciated the offer. 'Talk to you later.'

She went onto the forum to type in a reply.

I'm overwhelmed by everyone's kindness. Thank you so much. I'm going to be at the cinema most of the time, so do drop in and say hello if you're passing. I've got power and lights working now, so I can make you a cup of tea. And thank you again—all of you.

At five to eight, Patrick, Nicole's potential builder, arrived at the cinema. She made him a cup of tea and showed him round, explaining what she wanted to do with each room.

'That roof is stunning,' he said when he was at the top of the ladder in the upper room. 'Tin. That's not very common—but I know a guy who specialises in this stuff. The bad news is that he's booked up for months in advance, so you might have to leave the upstairs for a while until he can fit us in. Until you get rid of that lead paint, you're going to fall foul of regulations if you open it to the public.'

Just as Gabriel had warned her. 'I thought you might say that,' she said. 'The plan is, I want to use this room as a multi-purpose place—I'll have a proper screen so we can have a cinema, but also I want flexible staging so I can use it for a band and as a dance hall, or as a conference hall, or hire the room out to clubs or craft teachers.'

'Sounds good. What about the downstairs? With that mouse problem…'

'I've had the pest people out already and they've been back to check—they tell me that the mice are gone now,' she said, 'so it's just a matter of fixing the damage they've already done. But I'm not going to restore the seats quite as they are.' She explained about the sofas and tables.

'That sounds great. It'll be nice to see this place looking like she did back in the old days—or even better.'

It sounded, she thought, as if Patrick had fallen as much in love with the building as she had.

'You'll need a French polisher to sort out the bar, and there's a bit of damage to the glasswork that needs sorting out.'

'But it's all fixable,' she said. 'There is one other thing. I want it up and running in eight weeks.'

Patrick blew out a breath. 'You definitely won't get the upstairs done for then. Even downstairs might be pushing it—there isn't that much structural stuff, apart from the flooring once we've taken the old seats out, but there's an awful lot of cosmetic stuff.'

'I've, um, had offers of help from people who want to see the cinema restored,' Nicole said. 'If you have a site manager in charge, can they come and help?'

'Do any of them have experience?'

She grimaced. 'Um. Pass.'

'As I said, a lot of it is cosmetic. The more hands you have on deck, more chance you have of getting it done in your timeframe—as long as they do what the site manager asks and don't think they know better, it'll be fine,' Patrick said. 'So this is going to be a bit of a community project, then?'

'It looks like it.'

'They're the ones that make this kind of job feel really worthwhile,' he said. 'OK. I'll go and work out a schedule of works and give you a quote.'

'I hate to be pushy,' Nicole said, 'but when are you likely to be able to get back to me? This week, next week?'

'Given that you want it done yesterday—I'll try to get it to you for close of business today,' Patrick said.

She could've kissed him. 'Thank you.'

'No problem. And thanks for the tea.'

'Pleasure.'

When he'd gone, she went next door to see Gabriel.

'How did it go?' he asked.

She beamed. 'Patrick's a really nice guy and he loves the building. He's giving me a quote later today—and he's fine about everyone coming to help.'

'Sounds good.'

'I know I'm supposed to get three quotes, but I think I'd work well with him.'

'It's not always about the money. It's about quality and gut feel, too.' He gave her a hug. 'I still want to see that quote and the contract, though. Have you thought any more about furniture? The average retailer isn't going to be able to deliver you the best part of two hundred sofas in the next six weeks—they won't have enough stock. You'll need a specialist commercial furnisher.'

'I'm getting pretty used to eating humble pie around you,' she said. 'So if that was an offer of a contact name, then yes, please.'

'Better than that. If I introduce you, you'll get the same terms that Hunter Hotels do—which will reduce your costs,' Gabriel said.

'Is this how you normally do business, getting special deals for neighbours?'

'No. And it's not because you're my girlfriend, either. If we do the weddings and conferences, together, then if you use my suppliers I know your quality's going to be the same as mine. This is total self-interest.'

She didn't believe a word of it, but it made it a little easier to accept his help. 'It's really happening, isn't it?'

'Yes, it's really happening.' He kissed her. 'This is going to be amazing.'

Nicole spent the rest of the day finalising her lists for what needed to be done next, including applying for a wedding licence. Several people from the Surrey Quays forum dropped in to see her, some bringing photographs that she could borrow to have enlarged, framed and put on the walls in the reception area. She ran out of mugs and had to go next door to borrow some more mugs and coffee, to the amusement of Gabriel's team.

'So if you inherited this place from Brian… would your mum be Susan?' Ella Jones asked.

'Yes.'

'I always liked her—she was a lovely girl,' Ella said. 'Brian wasn't the easiest man. I always thought he was too hard on Susan.'

'He was but it was his loss, because my mum's amazing,' Nicole said.

'And so are you,' Ella's husband Stephen said. 'Most people would've thrown their hands up in the air at the state of this place and sold up. I bet him next door wanted this,' Stephen added, jerking his thumb in the direction of Gabriel's hotel, 'because the space would make a good car park for the hotel.'

'Gabriel Hunter's actually been really nice,' Nicole said. And if they knew he was Clarence… But it wasn't her place to out him. 'He's been very supportive. He's got a real eye for architecture and he sees the potential of this building, so he's working with me.'

'But that company—it just guts buildings and turns them into soulless hotel blocks,' Ella said.

'No, they don't. I've seen what he's doing next door and he's trying to keep as much of the character of the building as he can in the reception area, restaurant, bar, and conference rooms.'

Gabriel overheard the last bit of the conversation as he walked into the cinema foyer. And it warmed him that Nicole was defending him.

'If anyone here wants a tour next door, I'm happy to show you round,' he said. 'Oh, and since you pinched half my mugs, Nicole, I assumed you could do with some more supplies.' He handed her a two-litre carton of milk and a couple of boxes of muffins.

She smiled at him. 'I could indeed. Thanks, Gabriel.' She introduced him to everyone. 'They've lent me some wonderful postcards and photographs.'

'That's great,' he said. 'I'll go and put the kettle on and then take a look.'

Later that evening, he said to her, 'Thanks for supporting me when the Joneses seemed a bit anti. I thought you saw me as a shark-in-a-suit.'

'I know you better now. You don't compromise on quality and I think you'd be very tough on anyone who didn't meet your standards, but you're not a shark,' Nicole said. 'Oh, talking about being tough—Patrick emailed me the quote and contract. You said you wanted to look them over. How about I order us a Chinese takeaway while you do that?'

'Great,' he said. 'Let me have the surveyor's report as well, so I can tie them up.' He went through the documents carefully.

'What do you think?' she asked when he'd finished.

'Not the cheapest, but it's a fair price and he's been thorough. It matches what the surveyor said. And you said you felt he'd work well with you. I'd say you're good to go with your instinct.'

Once she'd signed the contract and agreed the work plan, a new phase of Nicole's life started. She ended each day covered in paint and with aching muscles, but she was happier than she could ever remember. She'd got to know more people from the Surrey Quays forum in real life, and really felt part of the community.

And then there was Gabriel.

They were still taking things relatively slowly, but she was enjoying actually dating him—everything from a simple walk, to 'research' trips trying different local ice cream specialists, through to dinner out and even dancing. If anyone had told her even six months ago that she'd be this happy, she would never have believed them.

The one sticking point was that Patrick's predictions were right and the ceiling specialist was booked up for the next few months. Gabriel had tried his contacts, too, and nobody was available: so it looked as if the grand opening of the Electric Palace was going to be the cinema only and not the room with the amazing ceiling. Weddings and conferences were off limits, too, until the room was ready. And now she'd finally decided to work with him, she wanted it all to start *now*.

'When you want something done, you want it done now, don't you?' Gabriel asked when she'd expressed her disappointment.

'You're just as bad.'

'True.' He kissed her. 'Maybe the dates will change on another project and the specialist will be able to fit us in, but even so we can still use the upstairs foyer as the café, the downstairs bar, and the cinema itself.'

'It's going to be done at some point. I just have to be patient.' Nicole stroked his face. 'You know,

I'm actually working longer hours than I was at the bank.'

'But the difference is that you love every second at the cinema.'

'I love seeing the changes in the place every day,' she said. 'And really feeling part of a team.'

'Part of the community,' he agreed. 'Me, too.' Other people had chipped in with information about the spice warehouse. 'And I've noticed that everyone's the same in real life as they are online. I wasn't expecting that.'

'And there's no snarkiness, nobody competing with each other—everyone's just getting on together and fixing things,' she said. 'I'm going to thank every single person by name on the opening night, as well as unveiling the board.'

'I'll supply the champagne to go with it,' he said.

She shook her head. 'You don't have to do that.'

'I know, but I want to. It's not every day your girlfriend manages to do something as amazing as this for the community.'

* * *

Nicole's mum and Jessie helped out at weekends and evenings, when they could. One evening, it was just the three of them working together, so Nicole ordered pizza when they stopped for a break.

'So when are you going to tell us?' Jessie asked.

'Tell you what?'

'About Gabriel,' Susan said.

'He's my neighbour, in business terms, and we have mutual interests. It's made sense for us to work together,' Nicole said.

Jessie laughed. 'And you're telling us you haven't noticed how gorgeous he is?'

Nicole couldn't help it. She blushed.

'So how long has this been going on?' Susan asked.

'Um.' She'd been thoroughly busted.

'You might as well tell us now,' Jessie said. 'You know we're going to get it out of you.'

Nicole sighed and told them about how she'd met 'Clarence' on the Surrey Quays forum and he'd turned out to be Gabriel. 'So the man I thought was my enemy was actually my friend all along.'

'But you're more than friends?' Jessie asked.

'Yes.'

'He's a nice guy. Not like Jeff,' Susan said.

'Definitely not like Jeff.' Jessie hugged her. 'You seem happier, and I thought it was more than just the job. I'm glad. You deserve life to go right for you.'

At the end of a day when Nicole had spent close to fourteen hours painting—and her arm ached so much she barely had the strength to clean her brush—Gabriel called in to the cinema.

'I wondered what you felt like doing tonight.'

'I don't think I'm fit for much more than a hot bath and then crawling into my PJs,' she said.

'I was going to suggest cooking dinner for us.' He paused. 'You could have a bath at my place while I'm cooking—and I'll drive you home afterwards.'

This felt like the next step in their relationship, and Nicole wasn't sure if she was quite ready for that. Her doubts clearly showed in her expression, because Gabriel stole a kiss. 'That wasn't a clumsy pass, by the way. It was the offer of a hot bath and cooking for you because you look wiped out.'

'Thank you—I'd appreciate that. But I'm covered in paint.'

'I could collect stuff from your place first. Or I could cook at yours, if you don't mind me taking over your kitchen,' he suggested.

'You'd do that?'

'Sure—and then you can eat dinner in your PJs. Which is again not a come-on,' he said, 'because when you and I finally decide to take the next step I'd like you to be wide awake and enjoying yourself rather than thinking, oh, please hurry up and finish so I can go to sleep.'

She laughed. 'You,' she said, 'are a much nicer person than you like the world to think.'

'Well, hey. I don't want people to think I'm a pushover, or negotiating contracts and what have you would be very tedious.'

'You're still a good man, Gabriel.' And maybe this wasn't just business to him; maybe he really did like her, she thought. He'd talked about taking the next step. It meant another layer of trust: but from what she'd seen of him she thought she could trust him. He wouldn't let her down like Jeff had.

In the end he made a chicken biryani for her in her kitchen while she soaked in the bath. 'I would normally make my own naan bread rather than buying it ready-made from the supermarket,' he said, 'but I thought in the circumstances that you might not want your kitchen being cluttered up.'

'It still tastes amazing. I don't cook much,' she admitted.

'Lack of time or lack of inclination?' he asked.

'Both,' she said.

'I love cooking,' he said. 'It relaxes me.'

She smiled. 'Are you going to tell me you bake, as well?'

He raised an eyebrow. 'I wouldn't rate my chances against a professional but I make a reasonable Victoria sponge.'

'You're full of surprises,' she said.

'Is that a bad thing?' he asked.

'No, because they're nice surprises,' she said.

Which told him that she'd had a nasty surprise from her ex at some point. She still wouldn't open up to him, but Gabriel hoped she'd realise that he wouldn't hurt her—at least not intentionally.

Georgygirl had been important to him. But Nicole was something else. The way he felt when he was with her was like nothing he'd ever experienced before.

It couldn't be love—could it?

He'd never been properly in love in his life.

But he liked being with Nicole. With her, he could be truly himself. The problem was, could she trust him enough to be completely herself with him?

'Tonight,' Gabriel said, a week later, 'we're going to see the stars.'

'That's so sweet of you, but there isn't long until the cinema opens and all the dark sky spots are way up in Scotland or near the border.' She wrinkled her nose. 'I'd love to go with you, but I can't really take that much time off.'

'Actually, there are places in London,' he said, 'right in the city centre. And tonight's the night when Mars is at opposition.'

'The closest it gets to the earth and it's illuminated fully by the sun, so it's at its brightest—hang on, did you just say there are dark sky places in the middle of London?' she asked, surprised. 'Even with all the street lights?'

'There's an astronomy group that meets in the middle of one of the parks,' Gabriel said. 'I spoke to the guy who runs it and he says we can come along—they have an old observatory and we'll get a turn looking through the telescope. So we get to see the stars tonight—but we don't have to travel for hours, first.'

'Gabriel, that's such a lovely thing to do.' She kissed him. 'Thank you.'

'You've been working really hard. You deserve a little time out and I thought you'd enjoy this,' he said.

The observatory was exactly as she'd imagined it to be, with a rotating dome and an old brass telescope. Just as Gabriel had promised, they had the chance to look through the telescope and see some of the features of Mars—and the moon, too.

Nicole loved it, and she loved walking in the park hand in hand with Gabriel afterwards. 'I'm blown away that you've taken the effort to do this for me,' she said. Jeff had never indulged her love of the stars, saying it was a bit childish. 'I feel a bit guilty that I haven't done anything for you.'

'Actually, you have,' Gabriel said. 'You've made me feel better about myself than I have in years—and I have some idea now of what I want to do in the future.'

'Such as?'

'I need to work it out in my head,' he said, 'but you're the first person I'll talk to about it.'

She grimaced. 'Sorry. I was being nosey.'

'No, you're my partner and it's nice that you're interested. Some of the women I've dated have only been interested in the depth of my bank account.'

'I hope you don't think I'm one of those.'

'Given how much hard work it is to persuade you even to let me buy you dinner,' he said, 'I know you're not.'

'So why did you date them?'

'I guess I was looking for someone who understood me. The problem was, the nice girls were wary of me—either they'd heard I was a wild child as a student, or they saw me as this ruthless businessman in the same mould as my dad. And the others weren't interested in understanding me.'

'So you're a poor little rich boy?'

'Yes.' He batted his eyelashes at her. 'And I won't make a fuss if you decide to kiss me better.'

She laughed. 'That's the worst chat-up line I've ever heard.'

'It was pretty bad,' he admitted.

She smiled. 'I'll kiss you anyway.' And she did so. Lingeringly.

Over the next couple of weeks they grew closer, falling into a routine of having dinner together most nights, and then Gabriel would take Nicole home and they'd curl up on her sofa together, holding each other close and talking.

'So do I ever get to see the bat cave?' Nicole asked.

'Bat cave?' Gabriel asked, looking puzzled.

'You've been to my flat. Yours is clearly the bat cave—top secret.'

He laughed. 'Point taken. I'll make dinner there tonight.'

His flat was in a very modern development, with a balcony running along the length of the building, and all the rooms faced the river.

'Bathroom,' he said, gesturing to the various doors as they stood in his small lobby, 'my bedroom and en-suite, main bathroom, living room, guest room.'

Like her flat, his had floor-to-ceiling windows, but his rooms were much bigger and so were the windows. Nicole adored the views.

The kitchen was just off the living room, and was about ten times the size of hers. It was clearly a cook's kitchen, with maple cupboards, worktops, and flooring. At the end of the living room, next to the kitchen, was his dining area; there was a large glass table with six comfortable-looking chairs. Three of the walls were painted cream, but the wall by the dining area was painted sky blue and held a massive painting of a stylised fish.

It looked like a show flat. And yet it also felt like home; the sofas looked comfortable, and she noticed he had the most up-to-date television.

'Home cinema?' she asked.

He nodded. 'But watching a film at home on your own isn't quite the same as going to the cinema with a group of friends. I think what you're doing to the Electric Palace is brilliant because you get the best of both worlds—all the comfort and all the social stuff as well.'

'I hope so.' The only thing Nicole couldn't see in the room was a desk. 'So you don't work at home?'

'The guest bedroom's my office,' he said. 'Though there is a sofa-bed in there if someone wants to stay over.'

He held her gaze for a moment. Would he ask her to stay over tonight? she wondered, and her heart skipped a beat.

She kept the conversation light while he cooked lemon chicken with new potatoes and she made the salad. But when they were lying on his sofa later that evening, he stroked her face. 'Stay with me tonight?'

She knew he didn't mean her to stay in the guest room. It meant spending the night in his bed. Skin to skin with him.

The next stage of their relationship.

Another layer of trust.

It was a risk. But the man she'd got to know over the last few weeks was definitely something special. Someone worth taking a risk for.

'I have a spare toothbrush,' he added.

She kissed him. 'Yes.'

And in answer he scooped her off the sofa and carried her to his bed.

A couple of days later, Nicole had some great news.

'My ceiling guy can fit us in,' Patrick said. 'The job he's working on has run into a bit of a legal wrangle, so he's got some spare time.'

'But doesn't he have a huge waiting list?' Nicole asked. 'Shouldn't he be seeing the next person on his list instead of queue-jumping me?'

'Probably,' Patrick said, 'but I've kept him up to date with what's happening here and he's seen the ceiling on your website. He says it's not a massive job—and also I think he fell in love with the stars and wants to be the one to work on it.'

'Got you,' Nicole said with a grin. 'Those stars really seem to do it for everyone.'

'I can't believe you've got all these people pitching in, too. I thought it was going to cost you an arm and a leg in overtime to get this done in your timeframe, but it's not.'

'No, but I do need to thank them. I'm going to have a board in the foyer with the names of everyone who's helped, and I'll unveil it on the opening night.'

'That's a nice idea.'

'I couldn't have done it without them,' Nicole said simply, 'so the very least they deserve is a public thank you.'

The person she most wanted to thank was Gabriel—for believing in her, and for being supportive. She just needed to work out how to do that.

'There is one thing,' Patrick said. 'Work on the ceiling means everything has to stop, because we can't do anything in that room until—'

'—the lead paint is gone,' she finished. 'Actually, that might fit in nicely.'

'Taking a holiday?'

'Sort of.'

She did some checking online, then called Gabriel. 'Is there any chance you can clear your diary for the next couple of days—preferably three?'

'Why?' he asked.

'That's on a need-to-know basis,' she said. 'I just need to know if it's possible.'

'Give me five minutes and I'll call you back.' He was as good as his word. 'OK, it's possible, but only if you tell me why.'

'It's a research trip. I could do with your views.' It wasn't strictly true, but she wanted to surprise him.

'All right. I take it that it's not in London, so do you need me to drive?'

'Nope. I'm borrowing a car. And I'll pick you up tomorrow at ten.'

It was a bright purple convertible Beetle, and Gabriel groaned when he saw it. 'You're going to tell me this is cinema-related because this is an update of Herbie, right?'

'I hadn't thought of that, but yes.' She grinned. 'Get in.'

'I thought you said my convertible was showing off?'

'Yeah, yeah.'

'So where are we going?'

'Road trip,' she said. 'Do you want to be Thelma or Louise?'

He groaned. 'This isn't going to end well.'

'Oh, it is. Trust me.'

She drove them down to Sussex, where she'd booked a couple of nights in an old fort overlooking the sea. She had a cool box in the back of the car filled with picnic food from a posh supermarket's chiller cabinet, and the weather forecast was good. This would be three days where they didn't have to worry about anything—they could just be together, relax and enjoy each other's company.

'Research?' Gabriel asked, eyeing the fort.

'Busted,' she said with a smile. 'I just wanted to take you away for a couple of days to say thanks for all you've done to help me.'

'It was pure self-interest. We have mutual business arrangements.'

'And I wanted to spend some time with you,' she said. 'Just you and me and the sea.'

'And an old fort—that's as awesome as it gets,' he said.

Three perfect days, where they explored the coast, ate at little country pubs and watched the sun setting over the sea. But best of all was waking up in his arms each morning.

Gabriel was everything Nicole wanted in a partner. He listened to her, he treated her as if her ideas mattered, he was kind and sweet and funny. And he could make her heart skip a beat with just one look.

The way she was starting to feel about him was like nothing else she'd ever known. She'd thought that she loved Jeff, but that paled into insignificance beside the way she felt about Gabriel.

But she couldn't shake the fear that it would all go wrong.

Everything had gone wrong when she'd moved in with Jeff. So, as long as they kept their separate flats and didn't say anything about how they felt, she thought, everything would be fine.

CHAPTER NINE

'I CAN'T BELIEVE how dim I am,' Gabriel said.

Nicole, curled up in bed beside him, just laughed. 'Dim is hardly the word to describe you. What brought that on?'

'The Electric Palace. We haven't looked in the film archives. And it's a *cinema*, for pity's sake. Moving pictures should've been the first place we looked.'

'Film archives? You mean, newsreels?'

'No. I was thinking of those Edwardian guys who went round the country taking films of everyday people,' he explained. 'They might have visited Surrey Quays.'

She looked at him. 'Actually, you're right, especially as your hotel was a spice warehouse—they specialised in factories, didn't they? So they're bound to have come to Docklands.'

Gabriel grabbed his phone and looked them up on the internet. 'Sagar Mitchell and James Kenyon. They made actuality films—everything from street scenes and transport through to sporting events, local industries and parades. The films used to be commissioned by travelling exhibitors, and were shown at town halls and fairgrounds.' He looked at her. 'And theatres.'

'If there aren't any films showing the warehouse or the theatre, we might still be able to find out if one of those films was shown at the Electric Palace—the Kursaal, as it was back then,' she said thoughtfully. 'That would be perfect for our opening night.'

'Have you decided what you want to show on the first night, yet?'

'I'd like one of the actuality films,' she said, 'and a classic film and a modern film, so we cover all the bases. Probably *It's A Wonderful Life*.'

'In July?' Gabriel looked surprised. 'It's a Christmas film.'

'It's brilliant at any time of year.' She punched his arm. 'Clarence, surely it'd get your vote?'

'Given your Surrey Quays forum name, what about *Mary Poppins*?' he suggested.

'We kind of did that on the beach in Norfolk,' she said.

'The first time I kissed you.' He kissed her lingeringly.

'You're an old romantic at heart,' she teased.

'Yeah.' He kissed her again.

'So, our classic film. Doesn't *Citizen Kane* top the list of the best films of all time?'

'Let's look up the list.' She did so, and grimaced. 'There are an awful lot on here I've never heard of, which is a bit pathetic for a cinema owner.'

'Let me have a look.' He glanced through them. 'I'm with you—haven't heard of most of these. And on opening night I think we need to have a broad appeal.'

'I did say I'd include some art-house evenings—I've been working on my scheduling—but I kind of want the film on the first night to be something I actually know. I'm standing by *It's a Wonderful Life*.'

'It's your show,' he said. 'And you're right. It's a good film.'

They snatched some time to visit the archives in the week. To Nicole's pleasure, there was footage of both the Spice House and the Kursaal—and they were able to arrange to use it for the opening night. Better still, they had permission to take stills they could blow up and frame for their respective reception areas.

'Luck's definitely on our side,' Nicole said. 'I think this is going to work out.'

'I don't just think it,' Gabriel said, squeezing her hand. 'I *know* this is going to work out.'

Nicole was working on a section of wall when she heard a voice drawl, 'That's definitely not how you used to dress in the office.'

Recognising the voice, she turned round. 'Hey, Neil—nice to see you. You might like to know that wall over there is partly thanks to the office.'

'Glad to hear it—I'll tell the team.' He glanced round the foyer. 'This is really impressive, especially when you see those pictures on your website of what it looked like when you took over. So I take it you're not planning to come and claim your desk back?'

'I hope not.' She smiled at him. 'Are you enjoying the view from my desk?'

'Considering I don't have it, no.'

She stared at him in surprise. 'But you were a shoo-in to take over from me while I'm away and then permanently if I don't come back. What's happened?'

'We had a bit of a restructure and the boss headhunted this guy—and if you come back I think this guy will be *your* boss as well.' He sighed. 'I was never going to like him much anyway, because he got the job that I thought would be mine, but even without that…' He grimaced. 'I just don't like Jeff. He isn't a team player. I mean, OK, so you never came out with us on team nights out, but we all knew you had our backs in the office, whereas he'd sell us all down the river. He'd sell anything to make a profit.'

Jeff. She went cold. Surely not? 'Would that be Jeff Rumball?' she asked, trying to sound as casual as she could.

Neil looked surprised. 'Yeah—do you know him?'

'I haven't seen him for a while, but yes, I know

him,' Nicole said. And the idea of failing to make the cinema a going concern and then having to go back to her old job, only to end up working for the man who'd betrayed her and left her self-esteem in tatters… Just no. It wasn't going to happen. 'My advice is to keep a low profile and to document everything. Copy things in to other people to be on the safe side, too,' she said.

'Got you.' Neil looked grim. 'We'd all rather you came back, you know.'

'Thanks for that,' she said with a smile, 'but I hope I'm going to make this place work.'

Although she chatted nicely with her former colleague and pretended to everyone else at the cinema that she was just fine, Neil's news left her feeling unsettled all day.

Jeff had used her to get ahead in his career. What was to say that Gabriel wasn't doing the same? Even though part of her knew she was being paranoid and completely ridiculous, she couldn't help the fears bubbling up—and Gabriel himself had admitted that he'd only joined the Surrey Quays forum at first to make sure he could head off any opposition to the development of the Spice House.

Eventually, sick of the thoughts whirling through her head, she left everyone working on plastering, painting, or woodwork, and walked to the café on Challoner Road to clear her head. She knew her mum was in meetings all day and Jessie was up to her eyes with her students in the middle of exam season, so she couldn't talk to them about Jeff.

Which left Gabriel.

Nicole had never actually told him about Jeff, but maybe this would be a way of laying that particular ghost to rest—and it would finally convince her that Gabriel was nothing like the man who'd let her down. She bought coffee and brownies, and headed for the Spice House.

But, as Nicole walked down the corridor to Gabriel's office, she could hear him talking. Clearly he was either in the middle of a meeting with someone or he was on the phone. What an idiot she was. She knew he was busy; she should have texted him first or called him to check when he might be free to see her for a quick chat.

She was about to turn away when she heard him say her name, almost like a question.

'Nicole? No, she's not going to give us any trouble, Dad.'

She went cold.

Jeff had used her to get on with his career. Right now, it sounded as if Gabriel was doing exactly the same. *She's not going to give us any trouble*—no, of course she wasn't, because he'd got her eating out of his hand. Over the last few months he'd grown close to her. He knew all her hopes and dreams; he'd made her feel that he supported her; and he'd made her feel that this thing between them was something special.

She'd thought he was different. After their rocky start, they'd learned to trust each other. They saw things the same way. They'd worked together to develop a conference package and a wedding package. She'd been so sure that she could trust him—with her heart as well as her business.

But that bit of conversation she'd just overhead made it horribly clear that it had all been to keep her sweet and to make sure that, whatever he really had planned for the Spice House, she wasn't going to protest about it.

So she'd just made the same old mistake. Trusted a man who didn't love her at all and saw her as a way of getting what he wanted in business.

Sure, she could go in to his office now, all guns blazing. But it wouldn't change a thing. It wouldn't change the fact that she was stupid and trusting and naive. It wouldn't change the fact that Gabriel was a ruthless businessman who didn't let anything get in his way. So what was the point in making a fuss? It was over. Yelling at him wouldn't make her feel any better. Right now, she wanted to crawl into the nearest corner and lick her wounds—just as she had with Jeff.

She should never, ever have opened her heart like this. And she'd never, ever be stupid enough to open her heart to anyone again.

Feeling sick, she walked away, dumped the coffees and the brownies in the skip, and then sent Gabriel a text.

I can't do this any more. It's over.

Then she walked back in to the cinema and pretended that nothing was wrong. She was smiling on the outside, but on the inside she was purest ice.

She would never, ever let anyone take advantage of her like that again.

'Dad, I love you,' Gabriel said, 'but right at this moment you're driving me crazy. I know that you rescued me from the biggest mistake anyone could ever have made and I appreciate that. But it was nearly ten years ago now. I'm not the same person I was back then. And, if you can't see that, then maybe I'm in the wrong place.'

'What are you saying?' Evan demanded.

'Dad, do you really expect your hotel managers to run every single day-to-day decision past you, so your diary and your day is completely blocked up, or do you trust them to get on with the job you pay them to do and run the hotels?'

'Well, obviously I expect them to do the job I pay them to do,' Evan barked.

'Then let me do the same,' Gabriel said. 'You put me in charge of the Spice House, and I've got plans for the place. And yes, they do involve Nicole—we're doing some joint ventures with her, so we can offer something that little bit different to our clients, both business and leisure. And she's using our suppliers.'

Evan snorted in disgust. 'Using our name to get a discount.'

'Using our suppliers,' Gabriel pointed out, 'so her quality standards are the same as ours. It makes sense. And yes, she gets a discount. That way we both win, and more importantly we get to offer our customers what they want. Which means they'll stay loyal to us.'

'I suppose,' Evan said, sounding far from convinced.

Gabriel sighed. 'Look, I know I did wrong when I was nineteen. But I've spent years trying to make up for it. If you can't move past what I did and see that I'm a very different person now, then there isn't any point in me working for you. I'll step aside so you can employ the person you need to get the job done.'

'Are you resigning?' Evan asked in disbelief.

'I'm pretty close to it,' Gabriel said.

'But it's the family firm. You can't leave. What would you do? Set up in competition with me?'

'I'd work in a different sector,' Gabriel said. 'Which is actually what I'd rather talk to you about. I'd like to work with you. But it needs be on my terms now, Dad. I can't spend the rest of my life trying to do the impossible because it's making us both miserable, and Mum as well. This has to stop. Now.' His mobile phone beeped, and he glanced at the screen, intending to call whoever it was back later. But then he saw the message.

I can't do this any more. It's over.

It was from Nicole.

What? What did she mean, it was over? Had something happened at the cinema—had Patrick found something unfixable? Or did she mean *they* were over?

He didn't have a clue. As far as he knew, he hadn't done anything to hurt her. So what was going on?

'Dad, I have to go,' he said swiftly.

'Wha—?' Evan began.

'Later,' Gabriel said. 'I'll call you later, Dad. Something's come up and I need to deal with it right now.' And he put the phone down before his father could protest. This was something that was much more important than sorting out his career with his father. He had no idea what the problem was, but he needed to talk to Nicole and sort it out. *Now.*

He found her in the cinema, wielding a paint-brush. Outwardly, she was smiling, but Gabriel could see the tension in her shoulders.

'Can we have a word?' he asked.

'Why?' She looked wary.

'We need to talk.'

'I don't think so,' she said.

So she *did* mean they were over. Well, surely she didn't think he was just going to accept that text message and roll over like a tame little lap-dog? 'OK. We can do this in public, if you'd rather.'

Clearly recognising that he'd called her bluff, she shook her head. 'Come up to the office.'

He followed her upstairs, and she closed the door behind them.

'So what was that message about?' he asked.

'All deals are off,' she said, 'and I mean all of it—the conference stuff, the weddings, and us.'

'Why?'

'Because I heard you talking to your father, telling him that I wasn't going to give you any trouble.'

He frowned. 'You heard that?'

'I was coming to see you about something. I didn't realise you were on the phone and then I overheard you talking.'

'Well, it's a pity you didn't stay a bit longer and hear the rest of what I said,' he said, nettled. 'What did you think it meant?'

'That you were planning something I wouldn't like very much, but I wouldn't give you any trouble.' She gave him a cynical look. 'Because I'm your girlfriend, so of course I'll flutter my eyelashes and do everything you say. You *used* me, Gabriel.'

'Firstly,' Gabriel said, 'you only heard part of a conversation—and I have no idea how you've managed to leap to the most incredibly wrong conclusion from hearing one single sentence. And, secondly, I thought you knew me. Why on earth would you think I would use you?'

'Because my judgement in men is rubbish—and I've managed to pick yet another man who'd try to leverage our relationship for the sake of his career.'

'If anyone else had insulted me like that,' he said, 'I would be shredding them into little tiny bits right now. I've already worked out that your ex hurt you pretty badly and you won't talk about it, even to me—but now you get a choice. Either you tell me everything yourself, right now, or I'll go and talk to your mum and Jessie. And, because they love you, they will most definitely spill the beans to me.'

'So now you're throwing your weight about and threatening me?'

'No. I'm trying to find out why the hell you're acting as if you're totally deranged, and assigning motives to me that I wouldn't have in a million years,' he snapped. 'If you'd bothered to stay and overhear the rest of the conversation, Nicole, you would've heard me telling my father that we're working together on conferences and weddings, and everything's fine because we're using the same suppliers and we have the same attitudes towards our customers—and that if he can't move on from my past and see me as I am now, then maybe it's time for me to step aside and he finds the person he wants to run the show and I'll go and do something that makes me happy.'

Understanding dawned in her eyes. 'So you're not…?'

'No,' he said, 'I'm not planning to do anything underhand. That's not how I operate. I'm not planning to put sneaky clauses in our contract in such teensy, tiny print that you can't read them and then you'll be so far in debt to me that the only way out is to give me the cinema. I thought we were working together, Nicole. I thought we were friends. Lovers. I've been happier these last few weeks than I've ever been in my life—because I'm with you. So what the hell has gone wrong?'

She closed her eyes. 'I…'

'Tell me, Nicole, because I really can't see it for myself. What have I done?'

'It's not you—it's me,' she said miserably.

'And that's the coward's way out. The way the guy dumps the girl without having to tell her what the real problem is. You're not a coward, Nicole. You're brave, you're tenacious, you make things work out—so tell me the truth.'

Nicole knew she didn't have any choice now. She'd let her fears get the better of her and she'd misjudged Gabriel so badly it was untrue. And she wouldn't blame him if he didn't want anything to do with her, ever again, after this.

'It's about Jeff,' she said. 'I'm ashamed of myself.'

He said nothing, clearly not letting her off the hook. Which was what she deserved, she knew. She took a deep breath. 'I didn't often go to parties when I started work. I was focused on studying for my professional exams and doing well at my job. I wanted to get on, to make something of myself. But four years ago I gave in to someone nagging me in the office and I went to a party.

And that's where I met Jeff. He was in banking, too—he worked for a different company, so I hadn't met him before. He was bright and sparkly, and I couldn't believe he could be interested in someone as boring and mousy as me. But we started dating.'

And what a fool she'd been.

'Go on,' Gabriel said. But his voice was gentler, this time. Not judging her.

Not that he needed to judge her. She'd already done that and found herself severely wanting.

'He asked me to move in with him. I loved him and I thought he loved me, so I said yes.'

'And that's when he changed?'

She shook her head. 'We moved in together and he was the same as he always was. He tended to go to parties without me, but that was fine.' She shrugged. 'I'm not really much of one for socialising. Outside work, I don't really know what to say to people.'

'You don't seem to have a problem talking to people at the cinema—and you definitely didn't seem to have a problem talking on the forum,' he pointed out.

'That's different.'

To her relief, he didn't call her on it. 'So what happened?'

'I can't even remember why, but I ended up going to this one party—and that's when I found out the truth about Jeff. I was in the toilet when this woman started talking to her friends about her boyfriend. I wasn't consciously trying to eavesdrop, but when you're in a toilet cubicle you can't really block people's words out.'

'True.'

'Anyway, this woman was saying that her boyfriend was living with someone else but didn't love her. She was a boring banker, and he was only living with her because there was going to be a promotion at work, and he knew his boss was going to give the job to someone who was settled down. The woman he was living with was the perfect banker's wife because she was a banker, too. Except the guy had bought the big diamond ring for her—for the mistress, not for the boring banker.' She grimaced. 'I felt so sorry for this poor woman who clearly thought her boyfriend loved her, but he was cheating on her and just using her to get on in his career. But then the woman in the toilets said his name. How many bankers are there called Jeff, who also happen to be living with a female banker?'

'Did you ask him about it?'

'Yes, because part of me was hoping that it was just a horrible coincidence and there was some poor other woman out there being cheated on—not that I wanted to wish that on anyone, obviously. I just didn't want it to be true about me. But he admitted he was seeing her. He said that was the reason why he'd started dating me and the reason he'd asked me to move in, so his boss would think he was the right guy for the promotion.' She swallowed hard. 'Luckily I'd moved into his place rather than him moving into mine, so I packed my stuff and went to stay with Jessie until I could find a flat. That's when I moved here.' And she hadn't dated since.

Until Gabriel.

And she'd been so happy...but now she'd messed it up. Big time. Because she hadn't been able to trust him.

'Jeff sounds like the kind of selfish loser who

needs to grow up, and I bet that promotion went to someone else,' Gabriel said.

'Actually, it didn't. He's very plausible. He got away with it. I have no idea what happened to his girlfriend, and I'm not interested in knowing.'

'So what does Jeff have to do with me?'

She bit her lip. 'You know I'm on a sabbatical?' At his nod, she continued, 'I thought my number two would take over from me in my absence, but it seems there's been a restructure in the office. Neil—my number two—came to tell me about it today. A new guy's been brought in over him and will probably be my new boss if I go back. And it's the worst coincidence in the world.'

'The new guy's Jeff?'

She nodded. 'I was coming to see you and—well, whine about it, I suppose. And then I heard what you said. And it just brought all my old doubts back. It made me think that I'd let myself be fooled all over again, by someone who was using me to get on in business.'

Gabriel took her hand. 'I'm sorry that you got blindsided like that, but everyone makes mistakes. Just because you made a mistake trusting him, it doesn't mean that you can't trust anyone ever again.'

'I know that with my head,' she said miserably. 'But it's how I feel *here*.' She pressed one hand to her chest.

'I'm not using you to get on with business, Nicole. I never have.' He raked a hand through his hair. 'Actually I was going to talk to you tonight about the very first wedding in the Electric Palace and the Spice House. I thought it might be nice if it was ours.'

She stared at him. 'You were going to ask me to marry you?'

'You're everything I want in a partner. You make me laugh when I'm in a bad mood. You make my world a brighter place. I'm a better man when I'm with you. But…' He paused.

Yeah. She'd known there was a but. It was a million miles high.

'But?' She needed to face it.

'You need to think about it and decide if I'm what you want. If you can trust me. If you can see that I'm not like Jeff.' He gave her a sad look. 'I thought you saw me clearly, Nicole, that you were the one person in the world who knew me for exactly who I am. But you don't, do you? You're just like everyone else. You see what you want to see.' He dragged in a breath. 'Talk it over with your mum and Jessie, people you do actually trust. And come and find me when you're ready to talk. When you're ready to see me for who I am. And if you don't…' He shrugged. 'Well.'

And then he walked out of the office and closed the door quietly behind him.

CHAPTER TEN

IT WAS REALLY hard to wait and do nothing, but Gabriel knew that Nicole had to make this decision by herself. If she didn't, then at some point in the future she'd feel that he'd railroaded her into it, and it would all go pear-shaped.

Patience was a virtue and a business asset, he reminded himself. He had to stick to it. Even if it was driving him crazy.

The only way he could think of to distract himself was to bury himself in work. So he opened up a file on his computer and started outlining his proposal to take the business in a new direction. If his father wasn't prepared to let him do that, then Gabriel would leave Hunter Hotels and start up on his own. It was something he should probably have done years ago, but it was Nicole's belief in him that had helped him to take the final step and work out what he really wanted to do with his life. But did she believe in him enough to stay with him? Or had her ex destroyed her trust so thoroughly that she'd never be able to believe in anyone else?

He had no idea.

He just had to wait.

And hope.

Gabriel had walked away from her.

Nicole stared at the closed door.

Of course he'd walked away. She'd leapt to the wrong conclusions and hadn't even given him a chance to explain—she'd just thrown a hissy fit and told him it was over.

By text.

How awful was that?

He'd been the one who'd insisted on talking. He'd made her tell him about Jeff.

And he'd made it clear that she was the one letting her fears get in the way of a future. He'd said she was everything he wanted in a partner. That he wanted them to be the first people to get married in the cinema. But he hadn't tried to persuade her round to his way of thinking, or to make her feel bad about herself, the way Jeff had. He'd acknowledged that she'd been hurt in the past and she was afraid. And he'd said that she was the one who needed to think about it. To decide if he was what she wanted. If she could trust him. If she was ready to see him for who he really was.

He was giving her the choice.

And he'd advised her to talk it over with her mum and Jessie. He'd known this was something she couldn't do on her own, but he was clearly trying not to put pressure on her.

She grabbed her phone. Five minutes later, she'd arranged to meet her mother and Jessie in the park opposite Jessie's school, giving her enough time to nip home and change into clothes that weren't paint-stained and scrub her face.

Both her mum and Jessie greeted her with a hug. 'So what's happened?' Jessie asked.

Nicole explained about Neil's visit and her row

with Gabriel. 'He told me to talk it over with people I trusted,' she said. 'Well, with you two.'

'So talk,' Susan said. 'How do you feel about him?'

Nicole thought about it. 'The world feels brighter when he's around.'

'Do you love him?' Jessie asked.

'Isn't that something I should say to him, first?' Nicole countered, panicking slightly.

'He told you to talk it over with us,' Susan pointed out, 'so no. Do you love him?'

Nicole took a deep breath. 'Yes.'

'And is it the same way you felt about Jeff?' Jessie asked.

Nicole shook her head. 'It's different. Gabriel sees me for who I am, not who he wants me to be. I don't worry about things when I'm with him.'

'You said he was a shark in a suit when you first met him,' Susan said thoughtfully.

'You've met him, so you know he isn't like that. He's been scrupulously fair. The problem's *me*.' She closed her eyes briefly. 'I'm too scared to trust in case I make a mistake again.'

'Everyone makes mistakes,' Jessie said.

'That's what Gabriel said. But what if I get it wrong with him?'

'OK—let's look at this the other way,' Susan said. 'Supposing you never saw him again. How would you feel?'

Like she did right now. 'There would be a massive hole in my life. He's not just my partner—he's my friend.'

'So the problem is down to Jeff—because he was a total jerk to you, you're worried that all men are like that, and if you let them close they'll all treat you like he did,' Jessie said.

'I guess,' Nicole said.

'Which means you're letting Jeff win,' Susan said briskly. 'Is that what you want?'

'Of course not—and anyway, I let Gabriel close to me.'

'And did he hurt you?' Jessie asked.

Nicole sighed. 'No. But I hurt him. I overreacted.'

'Just a tad,' Susan said dryly.

'I don't know how to fix this,' Nicole said miserably.

'Yes, you do,' Jessie said. 'Talk to him. Apologise. Tell him what you told us. Let him into your heart. And I mean really in, not just giving a little bit of ground.'

'Supposing...?' she began, then let her voice trail off. She knew she was finding excuses—because she was a coward and she couldn't believe that Gabriel felt the same way about her as she did about him.

'Supposing nothing,' Susan said. 'That's your only option, if you really want him in your life. Total honesty.'

'You're right,' she said finally. 'I need to apologise and tell him how I really feel about him.' And she'd have to make that leap of faith and trust that it wasn't too late.

Gabriel looked up when he heard the knock on his office door, hoping it was Nicole, and tried not to let the disappointment show on his face when he saw his father standing in the doorway.

'I didn't expect to see you,' he said.

Evan scowled. 'You said you'd call me back, and you didn't.'

The last thing Gabriel wanted right now was

a fight. 'I'm sorry,' he said tiredly, and raked a hand through his hair. 'I got caught up in something.'

'I'm not criticising you,' Evan said, surprising him. 'I was thinking I'd pushed you too far.' He looked Gabriel straight in the eye. 'We need to talk.'

'Yes, we do.' And this conversation had been a very long time coming. Gabriel paused. 'Do you want a coffee or something?'

'No.'

'OK. I'll tell Janey to hold my calls and I'm not interruptible for the time being.'

When Gabriel came back from seeing his PA, his father was staring out of the window. 'I see the cinema's nearly finished,' Evan remarked.

'Yes. It's a matter of restoring the sun ray on the half-moon outside and redoing the sign and that's it. It's pretty much done indoors, too.' He looked at his father. 'So what's this really about, Dad?'

'Sit down.'

Gabriel compromised by leaning against the edge of his desk.

'I owe you an apology.'

Now he knew why his father had told him to sit down—not to be bossy but to save him from falling over in shock. 'An apology?' He kept his voice very bland so he didn't start another row.

'What you said on the phone—you were right. Your mistake was nearly ten years ago and you're not the same person you were back then. You've grown up.'

'I'm glad you can see that now.'

Evan grimaced. 'I had you on speakerphone at the time. Your mother might have overheard some of what you said.'

Gabriel hid a smile. 'Mum nagged you into apologising?'

'Your mother doesn't nag. She just pointed a few things out to me. All the decisions you've made—some of them I wasn't so sure about at the time, but they've all come good. You have an astute business mind.'

Compliments from his father? Maybe he was dreaming. Surreptitiously, he pinched himself; it hurt, so he knew he really was awake.

'I saw that,' Evan said. 'Am I that much of a monster?'

'As a boss or as a father? And do you really have to ask?'

Evan sighed. 'I just worried about you, that if I wasn't on your case you might slip back into your old ways.'

'Maybe that was a possibility when I was twenty, but I'm not that far off thirty now—so it's not going to happen. I've grown up.'

'I guess I need to stop being a helicopter parent.'

'That,' Gabriel said, 'would be nice, but I guess it'd be hard to change a lifetime's habits.'

'Are you really going to leave the company?'

'Right now, I can't answer that,' Gabriel said. 'It might be better for both of us if I did. Then I can concentrate on being your son instead of having to prove myself to you over and over again at work.'

'You said about taking the business in a new direction. What did you have in mind?' Evan asked.

'We already have the hotels,' Gabriel said, 'for both business and leisure. The logical next step would be to offer holiday stays with a difference.'

'What sort of difference?'

'Quirky properties. Lighthouses, follies, water towers—places with heritage. Think somewhere like Lundy Island.'

'Old places that need restoring carefully?'

Gabriel nodded. 'That's what really interests me. I first started to feel that way when I did the Staithe Hotel, but working on this place and the cinema crystallised it for me.'

'Yes, I noticed you in a few of the photographs on the Electric Palace's website.'

Gabriel let that pass. 'This is what I really want to do. The way I want to take the company for the future. I like the research, looking up all the old documents and then trying to keep the heritage as intact as possible while making the building function well in modern terms. Fitting it all together.' He smiled. 'Hunters' Heritage Holidays. It's not the best title, but it'll do as a working one.'

'You've done a proposal with full costings?'

'Most of it's in my head at the moment,' Gabriel admitted, 'but I've made a start on typing it up.'

'You see things clearly,' Evan said. 'That's a good skill to have. I'd be very stupid to let that skill go elsewhere. And diversification is always a good business strategy.'

'So you'll consider it?'

'Make the case,' Evan said.

But this time Gabriel knew he'd only have to make the case once. He wouldn't have to prove it over and over again, the way he'd had to prove himself ever since university. 'Thanks, Dad. I won't let you down.'

'I know, son.' Evan paused. 'So do I get a guided tour of the cinema?'

'Not today,' Gabriel said. 'I have a few things to sort out with Nicole. But soon.'

Evan actually hugged him. 'Your mother wants you to come to dinner. Soon.'

'I'll call her later today,' Gabriel promised. With luck, by then Nicole would've had enough time to think about it—and with a little more luck he'd be able to take her home and introduce her to his family. As his equal.

After Evan left, Gabriel spent the afternoon working on his proposal. The longer it took Nicole to contact him, the more sure he was that she was going to call everything off.

Or maybe a watched phone never beeped with a text, in the same way that the proverbial watched pot never boiled.

He was called to deal with an issue over the spa and accidentally left his phone on his desk. He came back to find a text from Nicole.

I'm ready to talk. Can we meet in the park by the observatory at half-past five?

Please let this be a good sign, Gabriel thought, and texted her back.

Yes.

Nicole sat on the bench near the observatory, trying to look cool and calm and collected. Inside, she was panicking. Should she have planned some grand gesture to sweep Gabriel off his feet? Should she have spelled out 'sorry' in rose petals, or bought some posh chocolates with a letter piped on each one to spell out a message? Should she have organised a helicopter to whisk them away somewhere for a sumptuous picnic on a deserted beach, or—

And then all the words fell out of her head when she saw Gabriel walking up the path towards her.

He was still wearing a business suit, but he was wearing sunglasses in concession to the brightness of the afternoon. And his expression was absolutely unreadable.

He'd given her nothing to work on with his text reply, either. Just the single word 'yes'.

Help.

This could go so, so wrong.

'Hi.' He stood in front of the bench and gestured to it. 'May I?'

'Sure.' She took a deep breath. 'Gabriel. I'm sorry I hurt you.'

'Uh-huh.'

'I've been an idiot. A huge idiot. Because I was scared. I got spooked, and I should have trusted my instincts. I know you're not like Jeff. I know you're not a cheat or a liar. I know you have integrity.'

'Thank you.'

She still couldn't read his expression. Was he going to forgive her? Or had he, too, spent the time apart thinking about things and decided that she wasn't what he wanted after all?

All she could do now was be honest with him and tell him how she really felt.

'You've been there for me every step of the way. Firstly as Clarence and then as—well, once we realised who each other was in real life, and you made me see that you're not a shark in a suit. And ever since I first met you online, you've become important to me. Really important. I know I've behaved badly. And I'll understand if you don't want anything to do with me any more. But I think the Electric Palace and the Spice House have a lot to offer each other, and we've done so much work on our joint plans—it'd be a shame to abandon them.' She took a deep breath. 'But, most of all, Gabriel, I want you to forgive me and give me a chance to make it up to you. I have to be honest with you—I can't promise that I won't panic ever again. The hurt from what Jeff did went pretty deep. It shattered my confidence in me. I find it hard to believe that anyone can even like me for myself, let alone anything more. But I can promise you that, next time I have a wobble, I'll talk to you about it instead of overreacting and doing something stupid.'

Still he said nothing.

'I love you, Gabriel,' she said quietly. 'And I don't know what to do about it. I can't turn it into a balance sheet or a schedule or a timetable. It's just there. All the time. I want to be with you. I know you've dated women who just saw you in terms of your bank account, but that's not how I see you. I don't need a huge rock on my finger or a mansion or a flashy car. I just want you. Gabriel Hunter, the man who loves the sea and the stars and very bad puns, who makes my heart beat faster every time he smiles, and who makes even a rough day better because he's *there*.'

'That's what you *really* want?' he asked.

She nodded. 'You told me to think about it, to talk it over with Mum and Jessie, and I have. You're what I want, Gabriel. You and only you. I trust you. And I see you for who you are—the man I want to spend the rest of my life with. If you'll have me. And you're right—it would be pretty cool if the first wedding at the Electric Palace and the Spice House was ours.'

He removed his sunglasses so she could actually see his eyes properly. 'Are you suggesting marriage?'

'Strictly speaking, you suggested it first,' she said. 'But a merger sounds good.'

'Hunter Hotels is my dad's business, not mine. We won't be going into this as equal partners,' he warned.

'Yes, we will. Because this isn't about money or property or business. It's about you and me. That's all that matters. I want to be with you, Gabriel. You make my world a better place and I'm miserable without you.'

'Same here,' he said, and finally he put his arms round her. 'I love you, Nicole. I think I fell for you when I read that first message on the Surrey Quays forum. I was horrified when I met you and realised that my private friend was my business rival.'

'Except we're not rivals. We're on the same side.'

'Definitely.' He kissed her. 'So will you marry me?'

There was only one thing she could say. 'Yes.'

EPILOGUE

Three months later

GABRIEL, DRESSED IN top hat and tails, walked out of the honeymoon suite at the Spice House Hotel. The suite he'd be sharing with his bride, later tonight.

Everything was ready in the Coriander Suite—the tables were beautifully laid out and decorated for the wedding breakfast.

The Electric Palace was all decked out for a wedding, too. The old cinema was bright and gleaming, the bar in the downstairs foyer perfectly polished with trays of glasses waiting to be filled with champagne, and the Art Deco windows restored to their full splendour. On the walls were the plaque Nicole had unveiled on the opening night—thanking every single member of the Surrey Quays forum who'd helped to restore the cinema—along with framed enlargements of the Kursaal in its heyday and framed posters for *It's a Wonderful Life* and *Mary Poppins*.

There was a garland of ivory roses wound round the bars of the sweeping staircase to the upper floor, and when Gabriel glanced inside the upper room he could see that all the chairs were filled apart from the front row, which was reserved for his parents, Nicole's mother, and the bridesmaid.

The ceiling looked amazing. Just as Nicole had imagined it, the tin was painted dark blue and the stars were picked out in gold. There was an arch in front of the cinema screen, decorated with ivory roses and fairy lights.

All he needed now was to wait for his bride to arrive.

He glanced at his watch. He knew she wouldn't be late—that particular tradition was one that annoyed her hugely. But he was pretty sure she'd arrive exactly one minute early. Just because that was who she was.

The very first wedding in the Electric Palace and the Spice House.

Not because they were using their wedding as a trial run for their businesses, but because the buildings had brought them both together and there wasn't anywhere else in the world that would've been more perfect as their wedding venue.

And at precisely one minute to two the wedding march from Mendelssohn's *A Midsummer Night's Dream* began playing, and Gabriel turned round to watch his bride walking down the aisle towards him, on her mother's arm.

Her hair was up in the Audrey Hepburnesque style she'd worn the night he'd first taken her out to dinner, and the dress had a simple sweetheart neckline with a mermaid train that would look spectacular spread over the staircase. She looked stunning.

But most of all he noticed the expression in her eyes—the sheer, deep love for him. The same love he had for her.

'I love you,' he whispered as she came to stand beside him.

'I love you, too,' she whispered, and they joined hands, ready to join their lives together.

* * * * *

MILLS & BOON®

Large Print – December 2016

The Di Sione Secret Baby
Maya Blake

Carides's Forgotten Wife
Maisey Yates

The Playboy's Ruthless Pursuit
Miranda Lee

His Mistress for a Week
Melanie Milburne

Crowned for the Prince's Heir
Sharon Kendrick

In the Sheikh's Service
Susan Stephens

Marrying Her Royal Enemy
Jennifer Hayward

An Unlikely Bride for the Billionaire
Michelle Douglas

Falling for the Secret Millionaire
Kate Hardy

The Forbidden Prince
Alison Roberts

The Best Man's Guarded Heart
Katrina Cudmore

MILLS & BOON®

Large Print – January 2017

To Blackmail a Di Sione
Rachael Thomas

A Ring for Vincenzo's Heir
Jennie Lucas

Demetriou Demands His Child
Kate Hewitt

Trapped by Vialli's Vows
Chantelle Shaw

The Sheikh's Baby Scandal
Carol Marinelli

Defying the Billionaire's Command
Michelle Conder

The Secret Beneath the Veil
Dani Collins

Stepping into the Prince's World
Marion Lennox

Unveiling the Bridesmaid
Jessica Gilmore

The CEO's Surprise Family
Teresa Carpenter

The Billionaire from Her Past
Leah Ashton